UNDERWATER MISSION

2 GRAPHIC ADVENTURES

Adapted by
Simcha Whitehill

An Imprint of
SCHOLASTIC

ISBN 978-1-339-02805-7

10 9 8 7 6 5 4 3 2 1   24 25 26 27 28

Printed in China   62

First printing 2024

Designed by Cheung Tai

CONTENTS

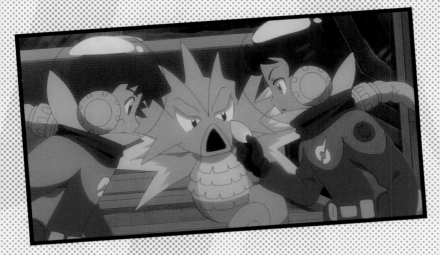

The Search for Kingdra

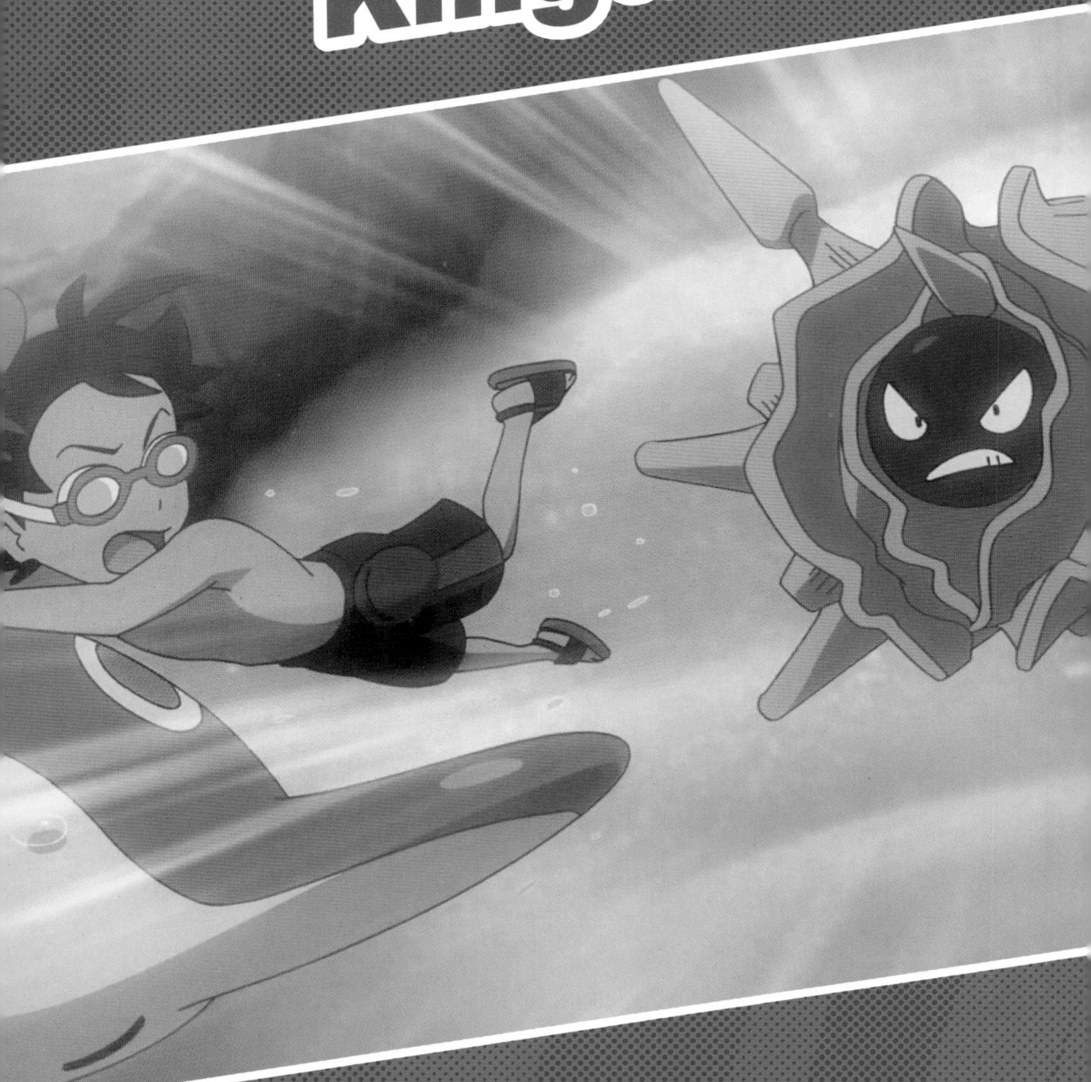

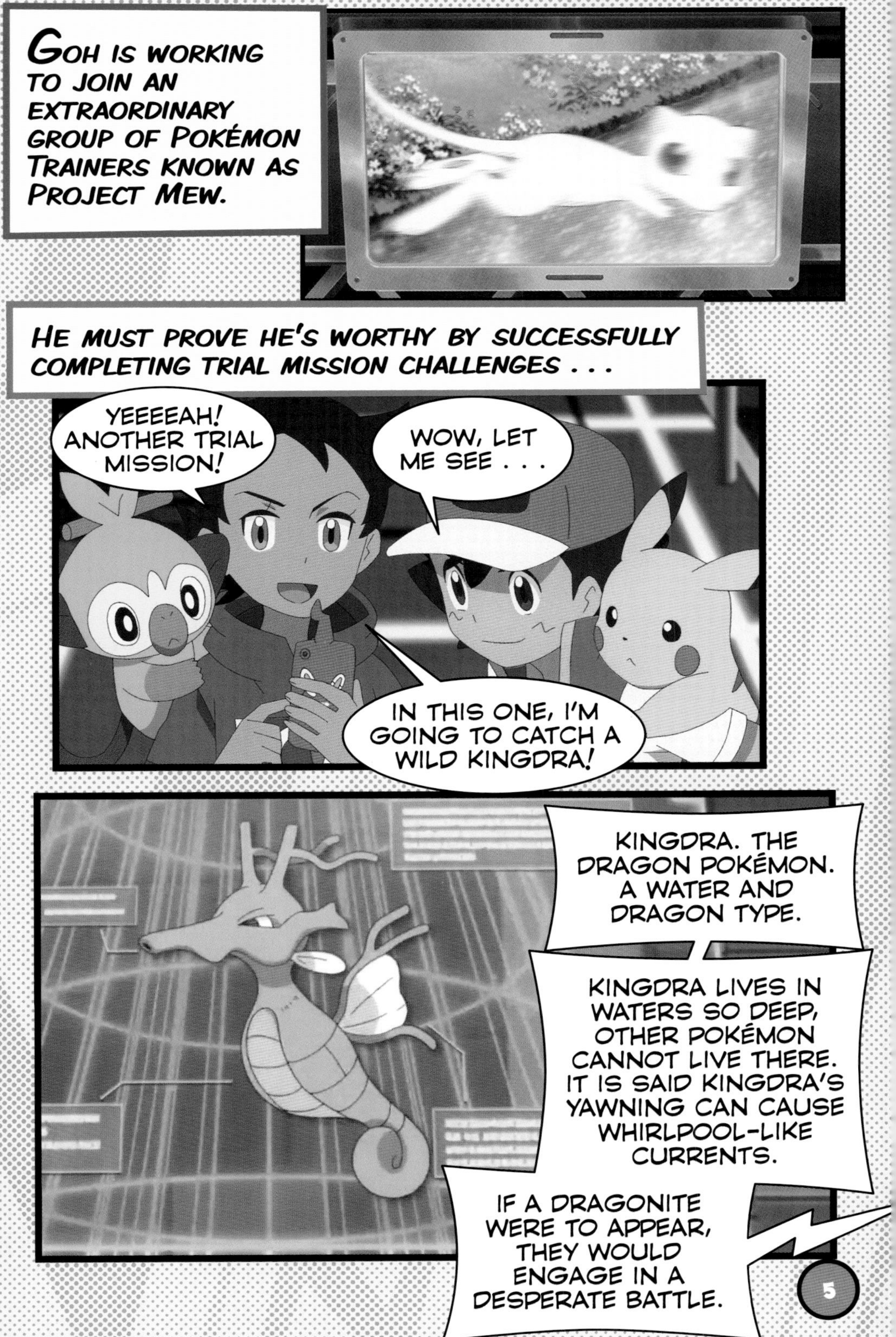

GOH IS WORKING TO JOIN AN EXTRAORDINARY GROUP OF POKÉMON TRAINERS KNOWN AS PROJECT MEW.
HE MUST PROVE HE'S WORTHY BY SUCCESSFULLY COMPLETING TRIAL MISSION CHALLENGES . . .
YEEEEAH! ANOTHER TRIAL MISSION!
WOW, LET ME SEE . . .
IN THIS ONE, I'M GOING TO CATCH A WILD KINGDRA!
KINGDRA. THE DRAGON POKÉMON. A WATER AND DRAGON TYPE.
KINGDRA LIVES IN WATERS SO DEEP, OTHER POKÉMON CANNOT LIVE THERE. IT IS SAID KINGDRA'S YAWNING CAN CAUSE WHIRLPOOL-LIKE CURRENTS.
IF A DRAGONITE WERE TO APPEAR, THEY WOULD ENGAGE IN A DESPERATE BATTLE.

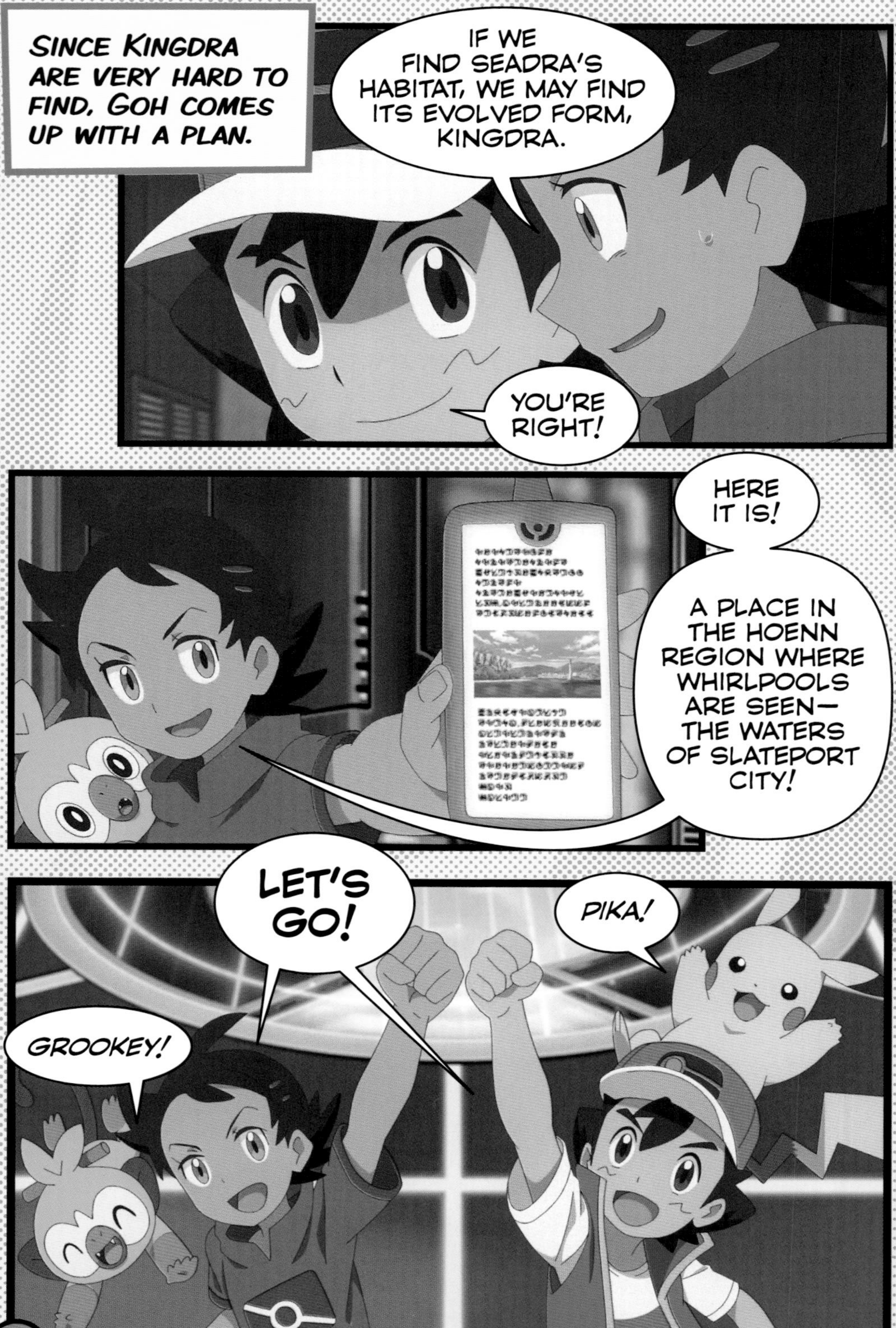
SINCE KINGDRA ARE VERY HARD TO FIND, GOH COMES UP WITH A PLAN.
IF WE FIND SEADRA'S HABITAT, WE MAY FIND ITS EVOLVED FORM, KINGDRA.
YOU'RE RIGHT!
HERE IT IS!
A PLACE IN THE HOENN REGION WHERE WHIRLPOOLS ARE SEEN—THE WATERS OF SLATEPORT CITY!
LET'S GO!
PIKA!
GROOKEY!

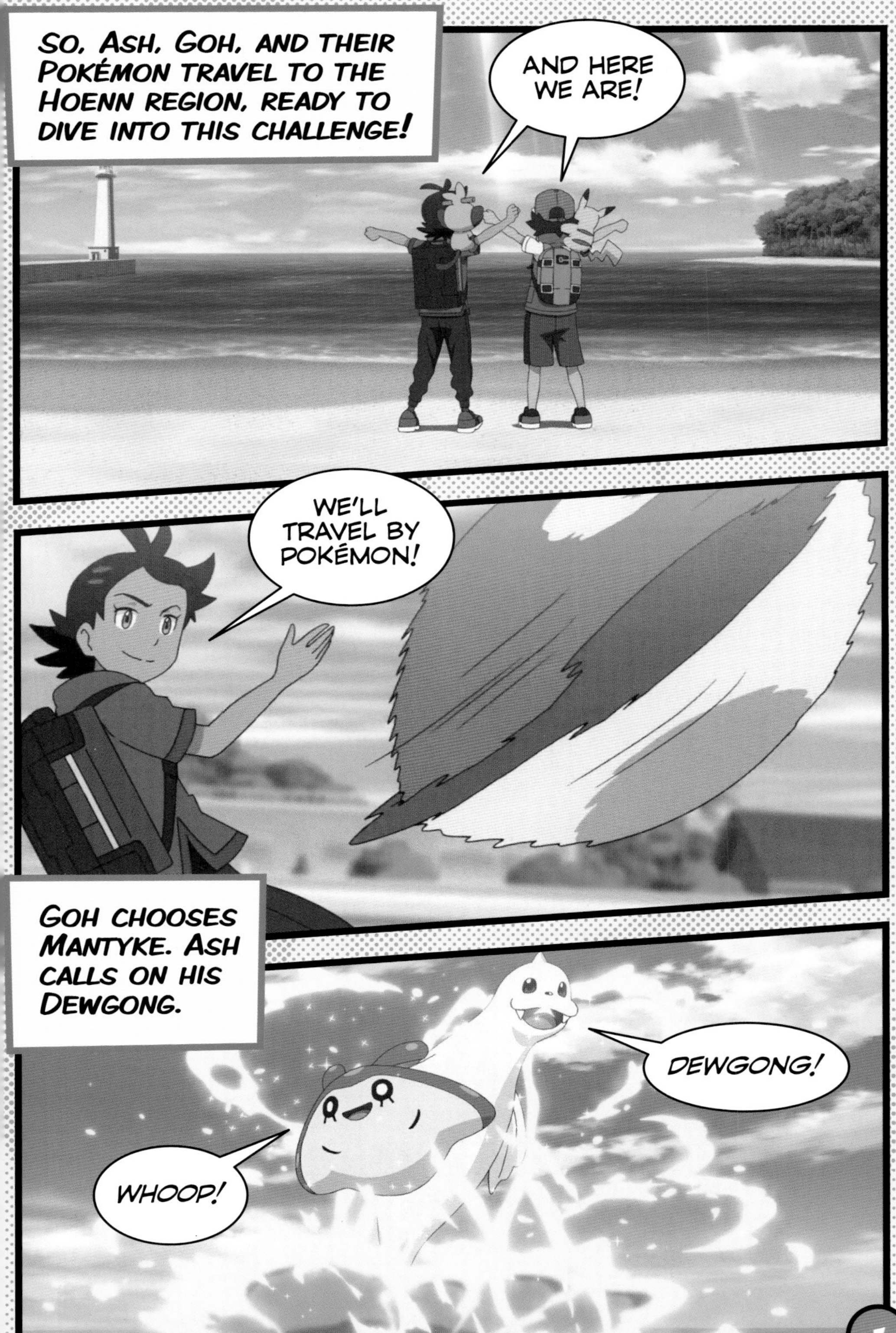
So, Ash, Goh, and their Pokémon travel to the Hoenn region, ready to dive into this challenge!
And here we are!
We'll travel by Pokémon!
Goh chooses Mantyke. Ash calls on his Dewgong.
Dewgong!
Whoop!

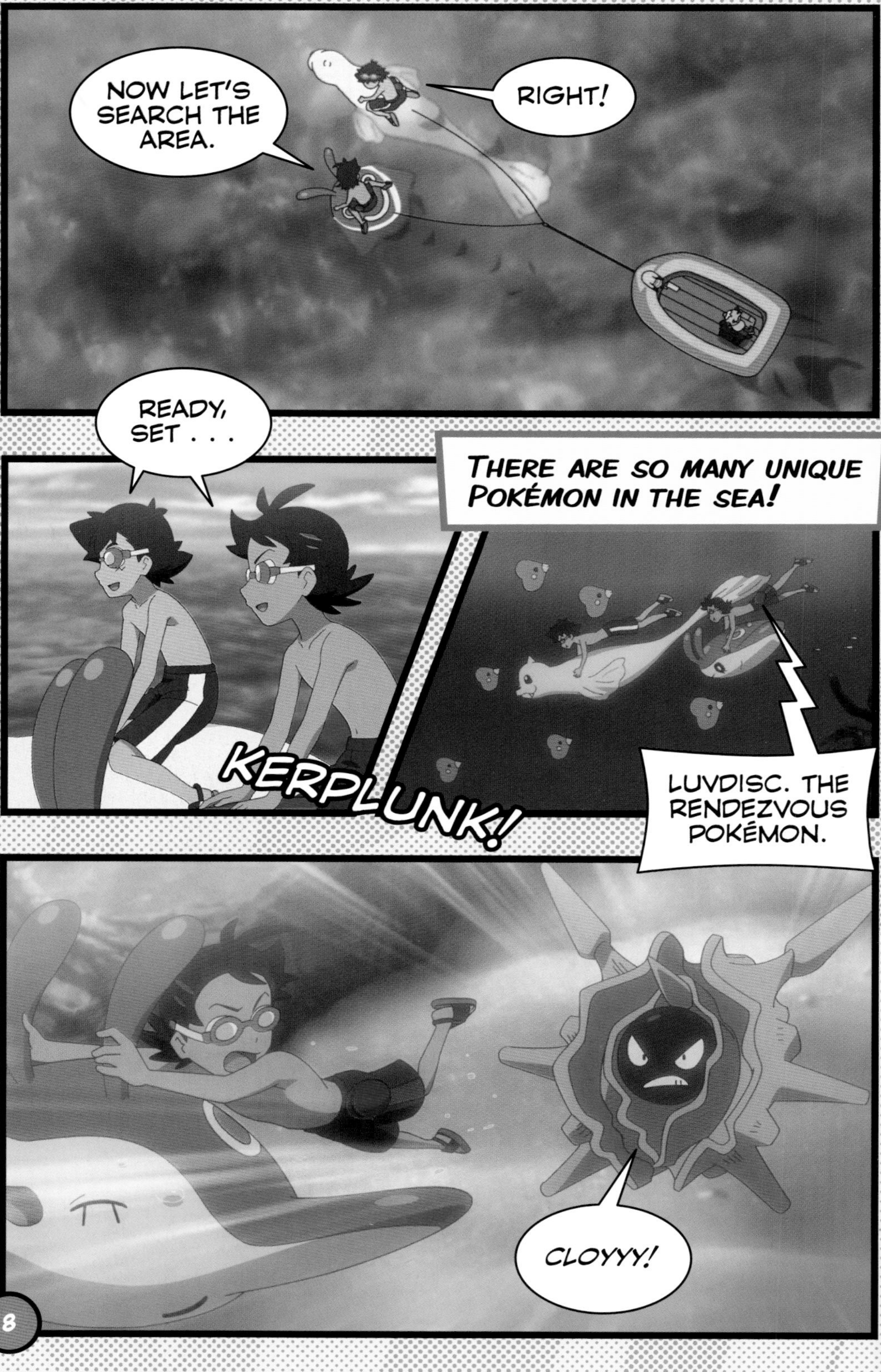

NOW LET'S SEARCH THE AREA.
RIGHT!
READY, SET . . .
KERPLUNK!
THERE ARE SO MANY UNIQUE POKÉMON IN THE SEA!
LUVDISC. THE RENDEZVOUS POKÉMON.
CLOYYY!

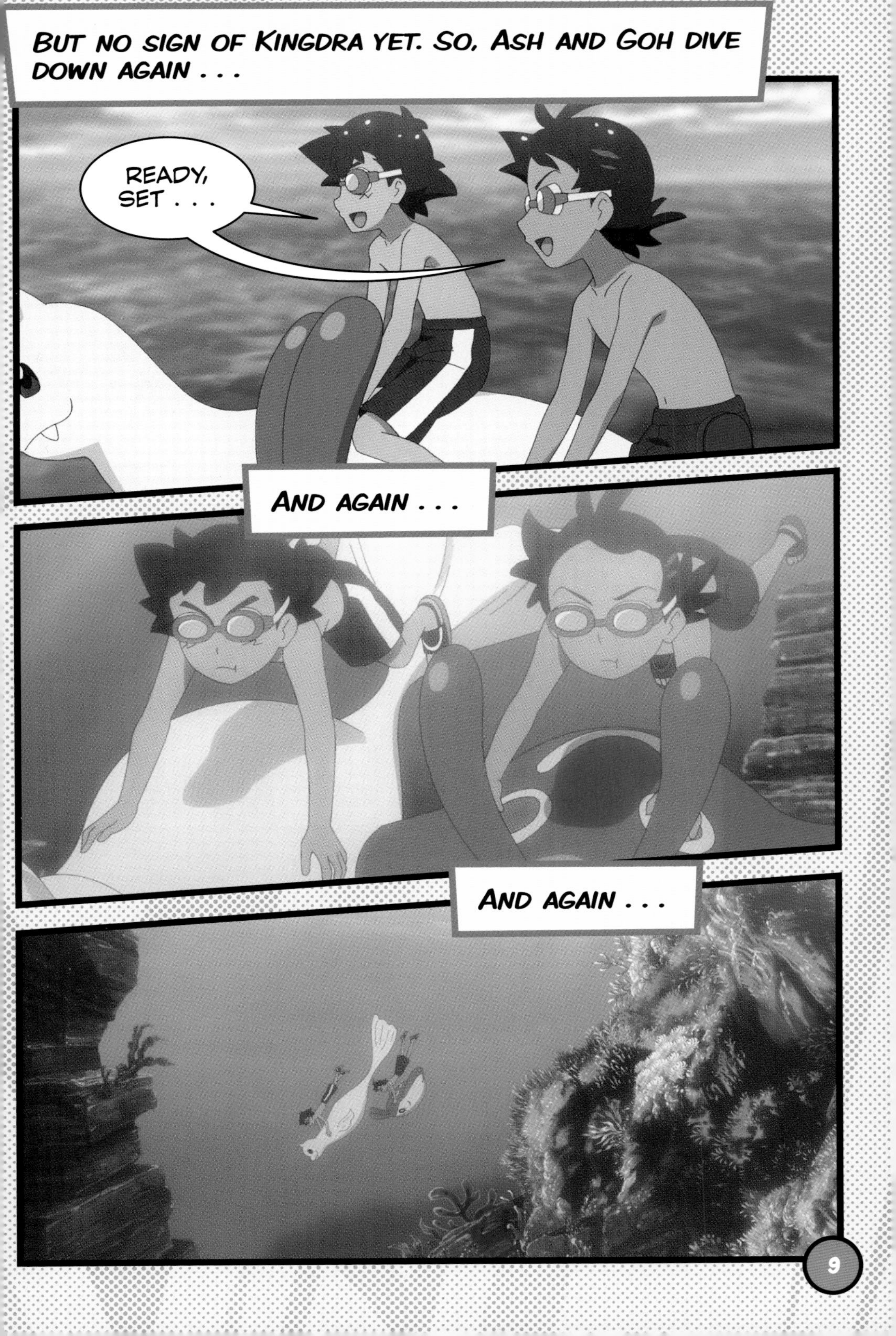
BUT NO SIGN OF KINGDRA YET. SO, ASH AND GOH DIVE DOWN AGAIN . . .
READY, SET . . .
AND AGAIN . . .
AND AGAIN . . .

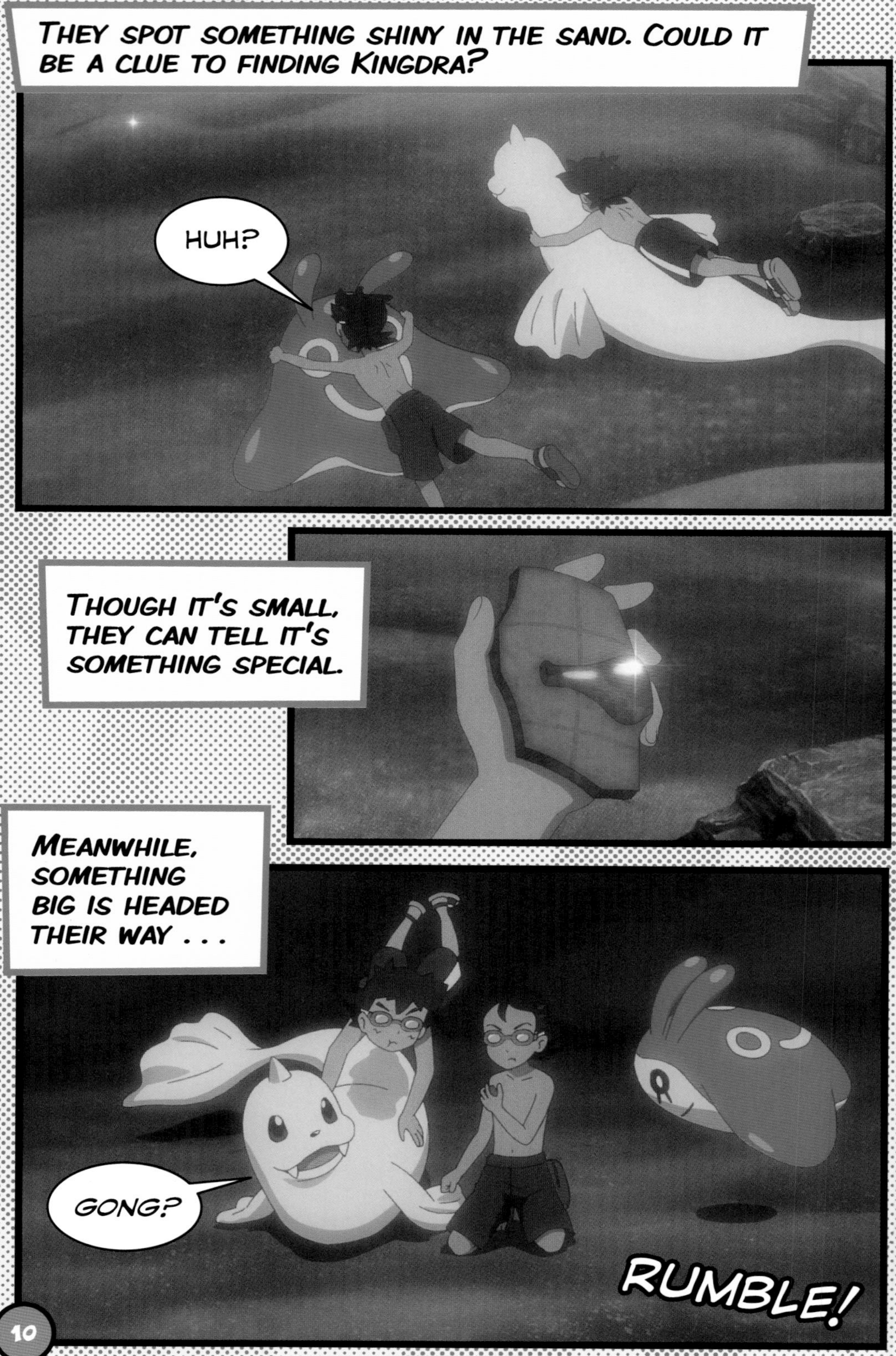
THEY SPOT SOMETHING SHINY IN THE SAND. COULD IT BE A CLUE TO FINDING KINGDRA?
HUH?
THOUGH IT'S SMALL, THEY CAN TELL IT'S SOMETHING SPECIAL.
MEANWHILE, SOMETHING BIG IS HEADED THEIR WAY . . .
GONG?
RUMBLE!

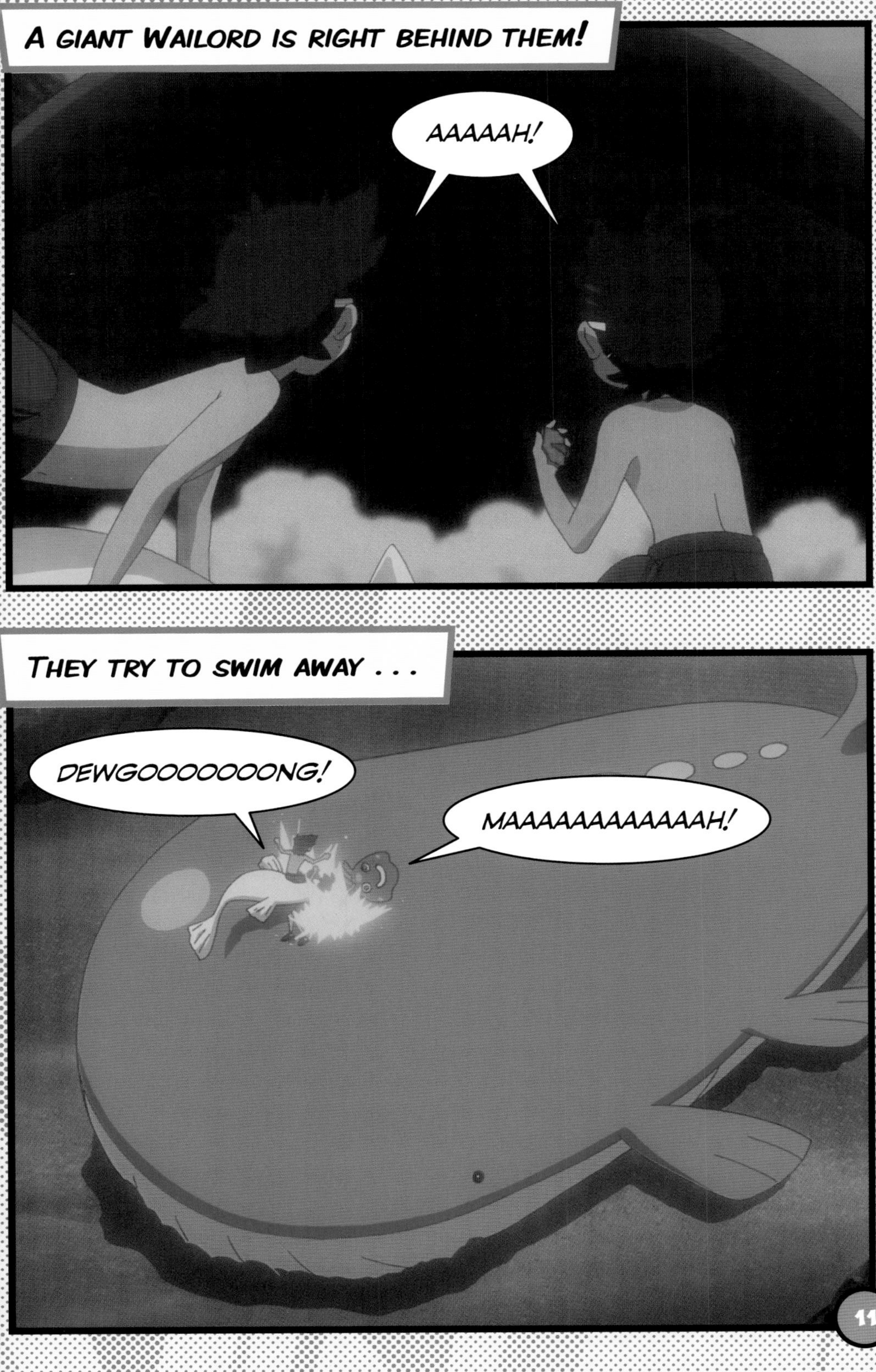
A GIANT WAILORD IS RIGHT BEHIND THEM!
AAAAAH!
THEY TRY TO SWIM AWAY . . .
DEWGOOOOOOONG!
MAAAAAAAAAAAAAH!

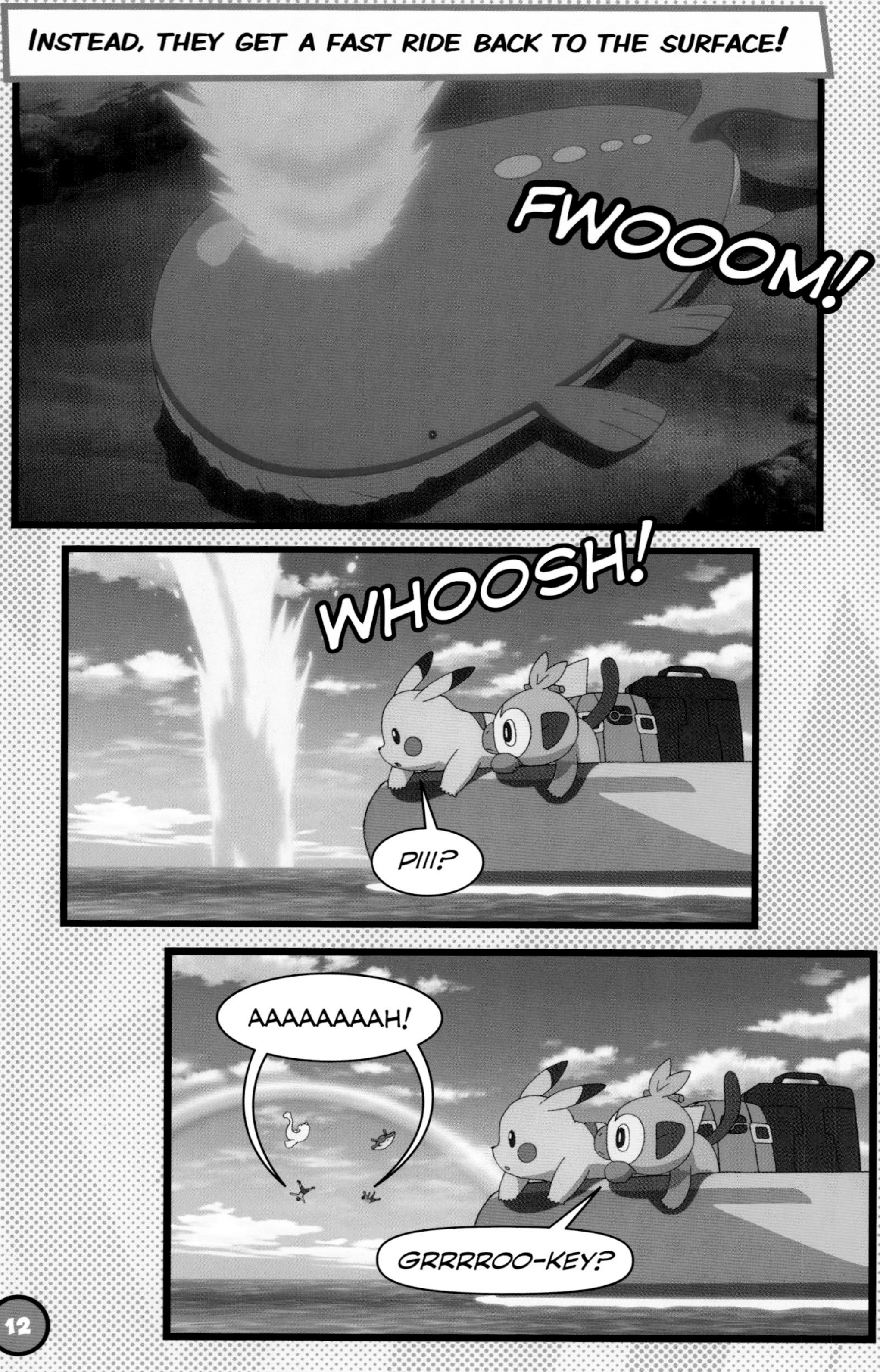
INSTEAD, THEY GET A FAST RIDE BACK TO THE SURFACE!
FWOOOOM!
WHOOOSH!
PIII?
AAAAAAAAAH!
GRRRROO-KEY?

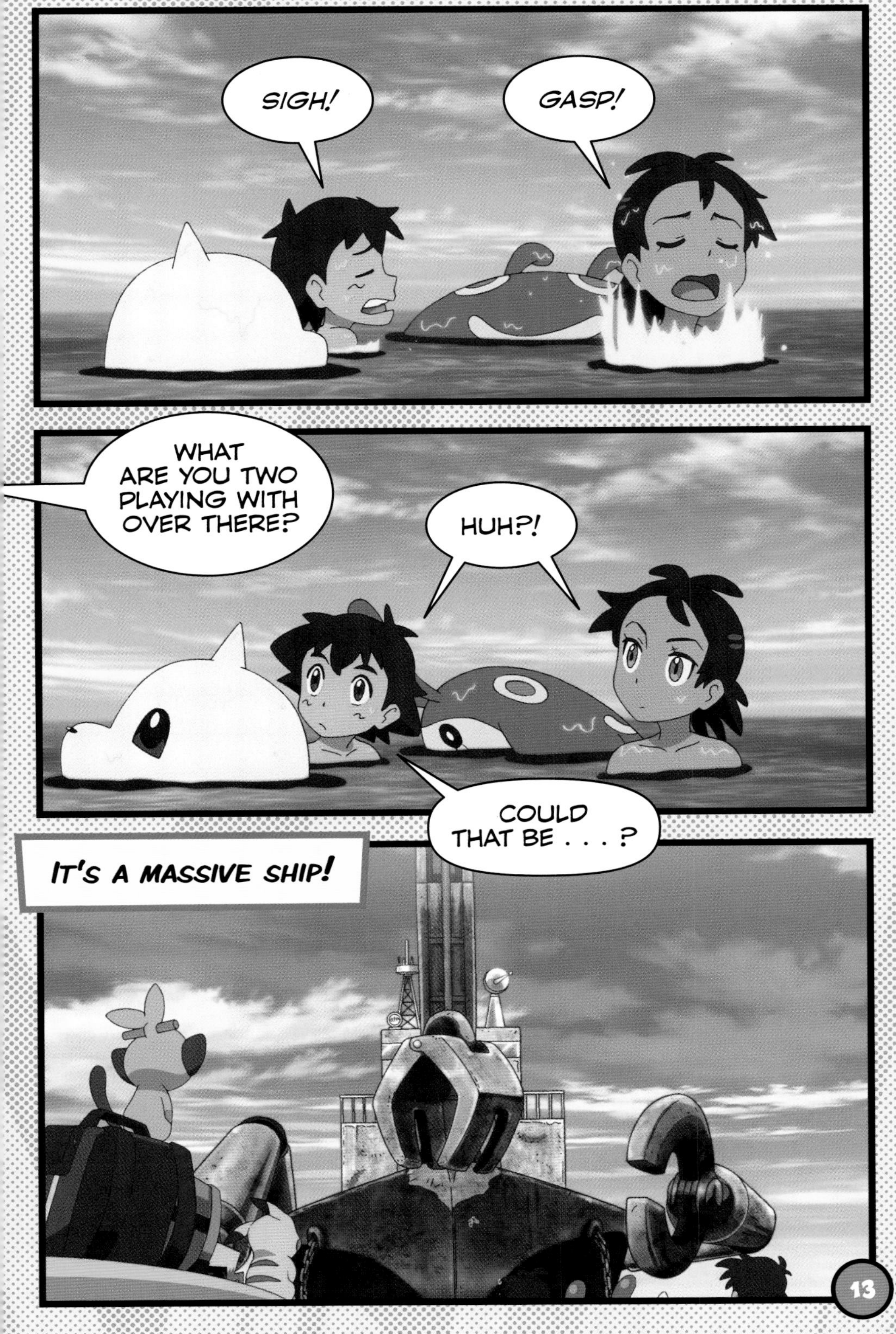
SIGH!
GASP!
WHAT ARE YOU TWO PLAYING WITH OVER THERE?
HUH?!
COULD THAT BE . . . ?
IT'S A MASSIVE SHIP!

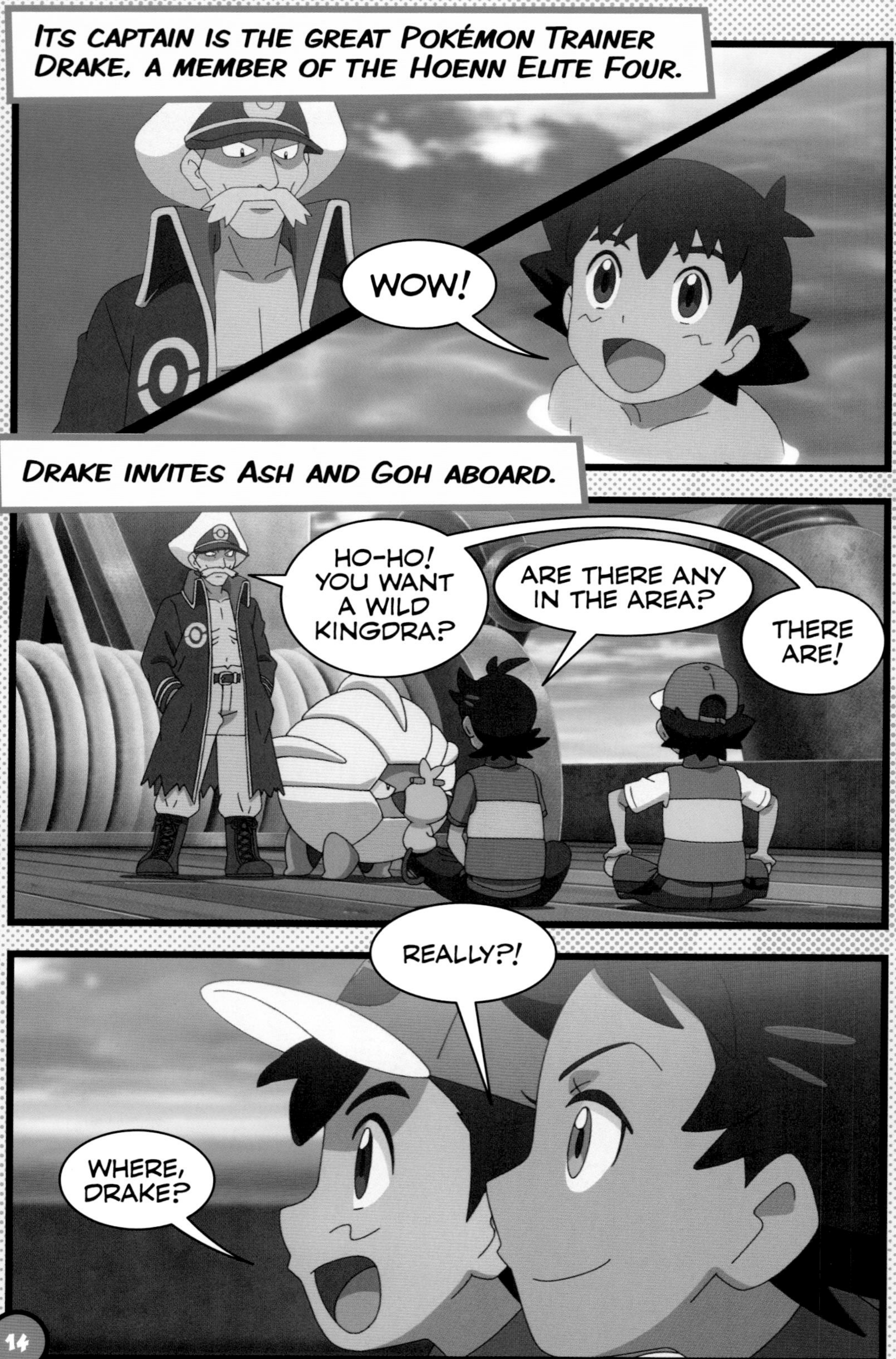

ITS CAPTAIN IS THE GREAT POKÉMON TRAINER DRAKE, A MEMBER OF THE HOENN ELITE FOUR.
WOW!
DRAKE INVITES ASH AND GOH ABOARD.
HO-HO! YOU WANT A WILD KINGDRA?
ARE THERE ANY IN THE AREA?
THERE ARE!
REALLY?!
WHERE, DRAKE?

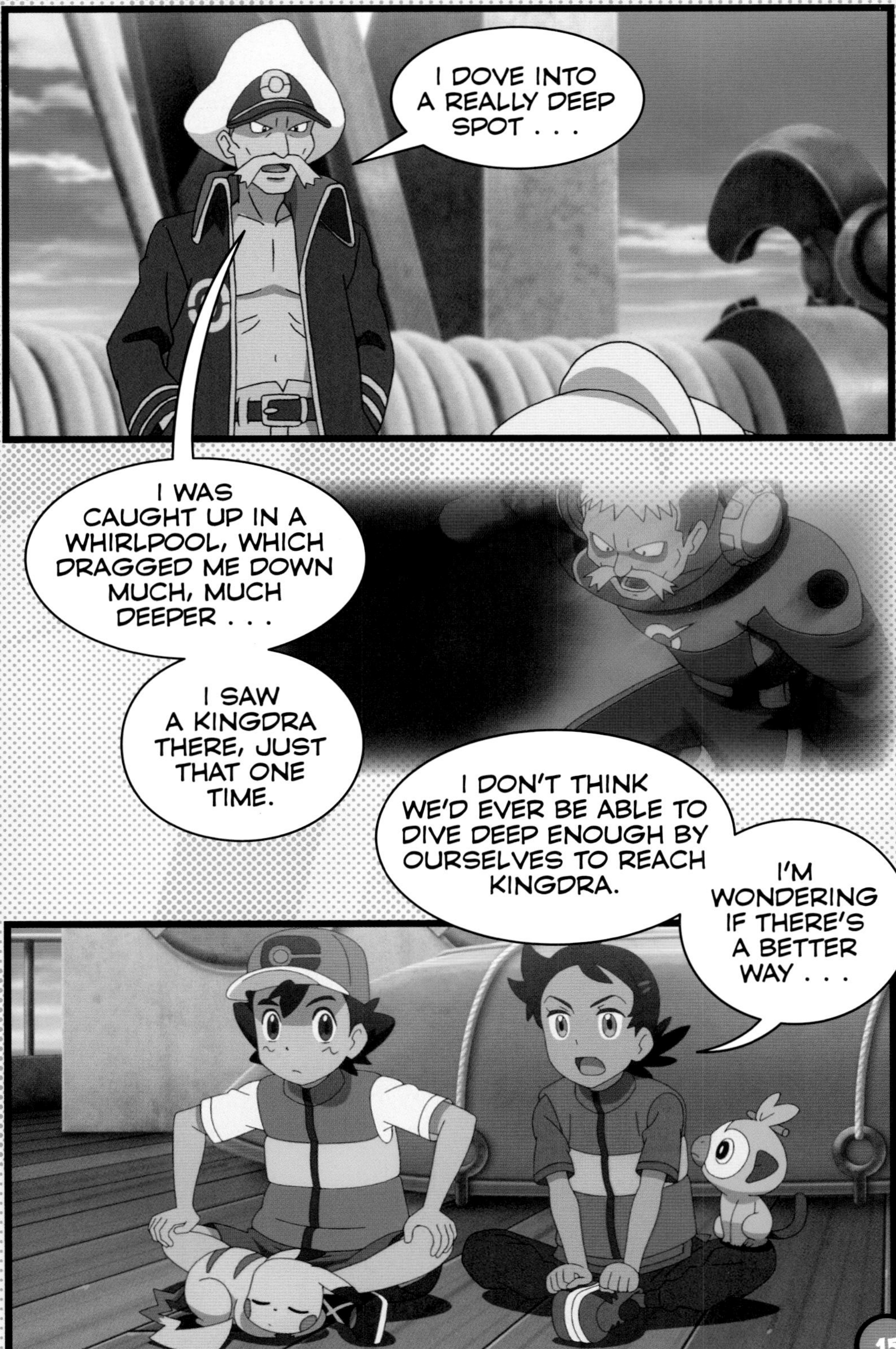
I DOVE INTO A REALLY DEEP SPOT . . .
I WAS CAUGHT UP IN A WHIRLPOOL, WHICH DRAGGED ME DOWN MUCH, MUCH DEEPER . . .
I SAW A KINGDRA THERE, JUST THAT ONE TIME.
I DON'T THINK WE'D EVER BE ABLE TO DIVE DEEP ENOUGH BY OURSELVES TO REACH KINGDRA.
I'M WONDERING IF THERE'S A BETTER WAY . . .

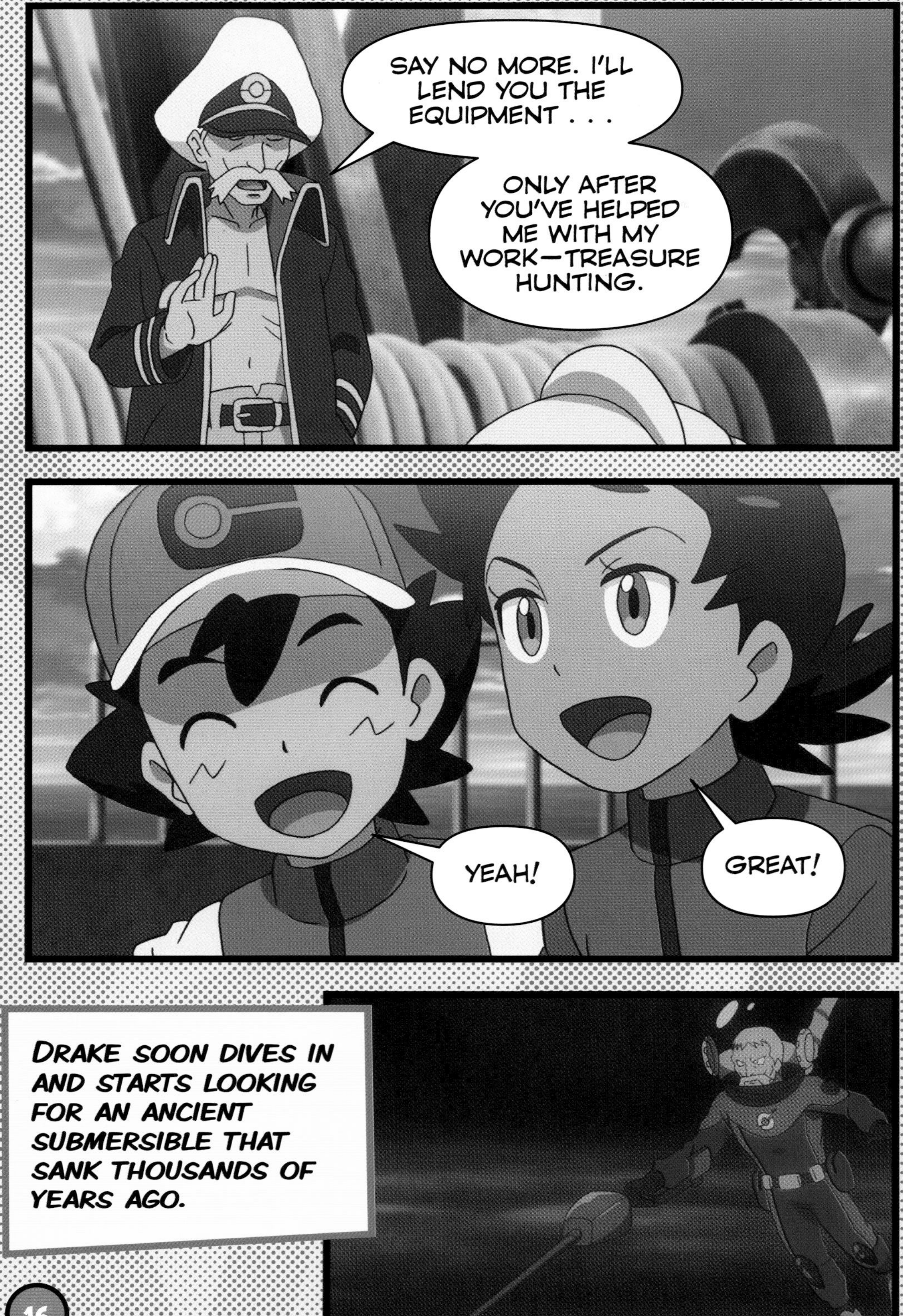
SAY NO MORE. I'LL LEND YOU THE EQUIPMENT . . .
ONLY AFTER YOU'VE HELPED ME WITH MY WORK—TREASURE HUNTING.
YEAH!
GREAT!
DRAKE SOON DIVES IN AND STARTS LOOKING FOR AN ANCIENT SUBMERSIBLE THAT SANK THOUSANDS OF YEARS AGO.

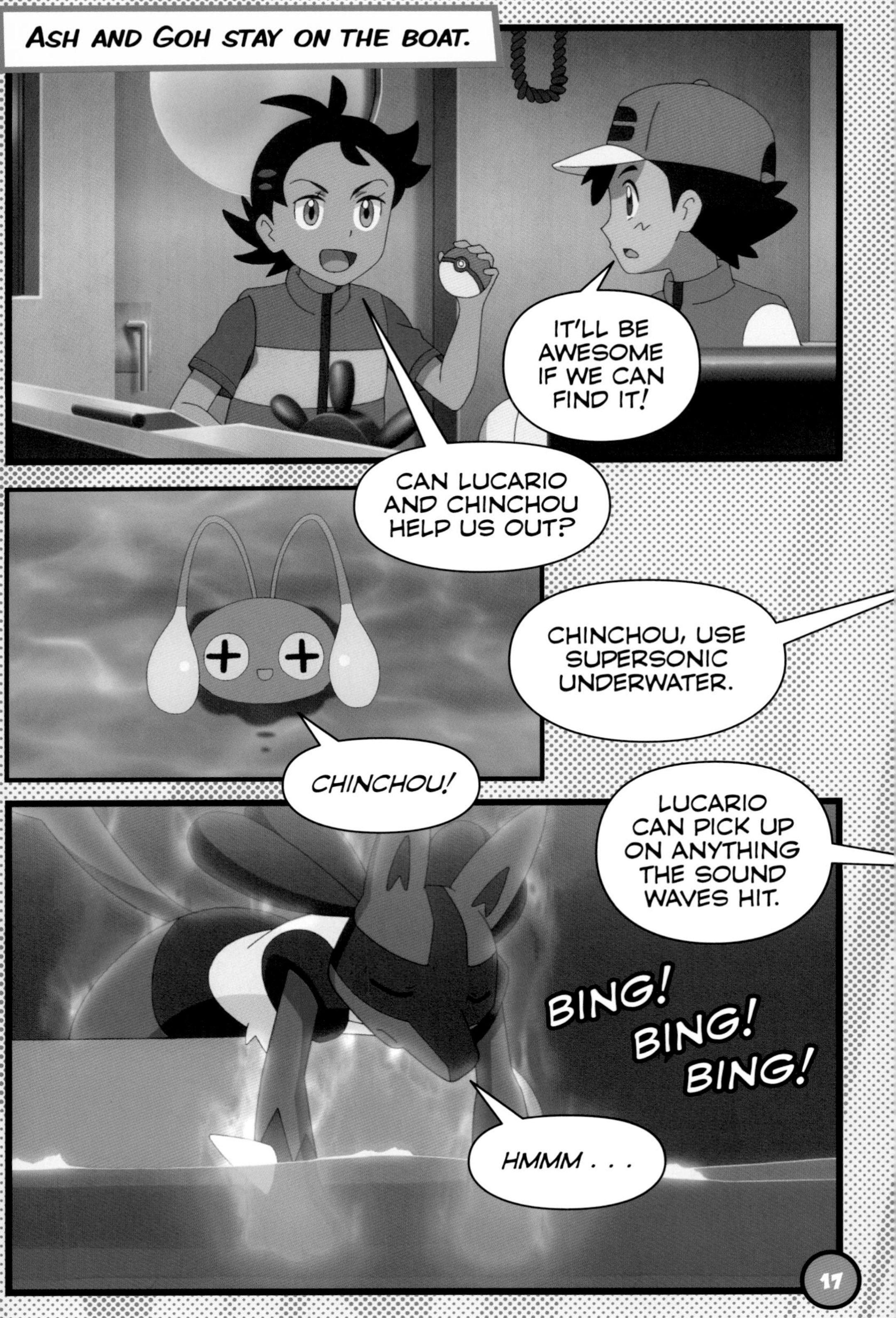
Ash and Goh stay on the boat.
It'll be awesome if we can find it!
Can Lucario and Chinchou help us out?
Chinchou, use Supersonic underwater.
Chinchou!
Lucario can pick up on anything the sound waves hit.
BING! BING! BING!
Hmmm . . .

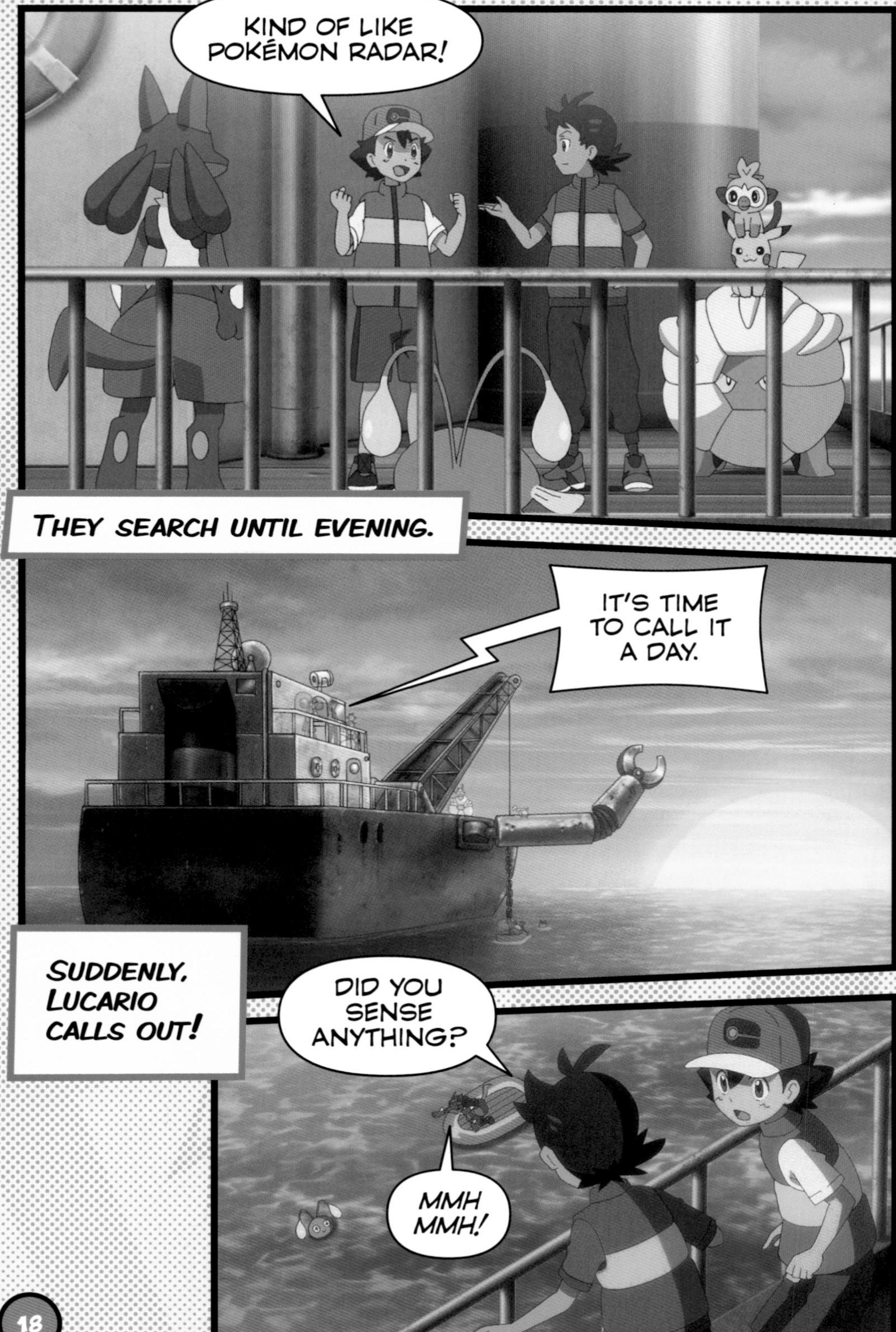
KIND OF LIKE POKÉMON RADAR!
THEY SEARCH UNTIL EVENING.
IT'S TIME TO CALL IT A DAY.
SUDDENLY, LUCARIO CALLS OUT!
DID YOU SENSE ANYTHING?
MMH MMH!

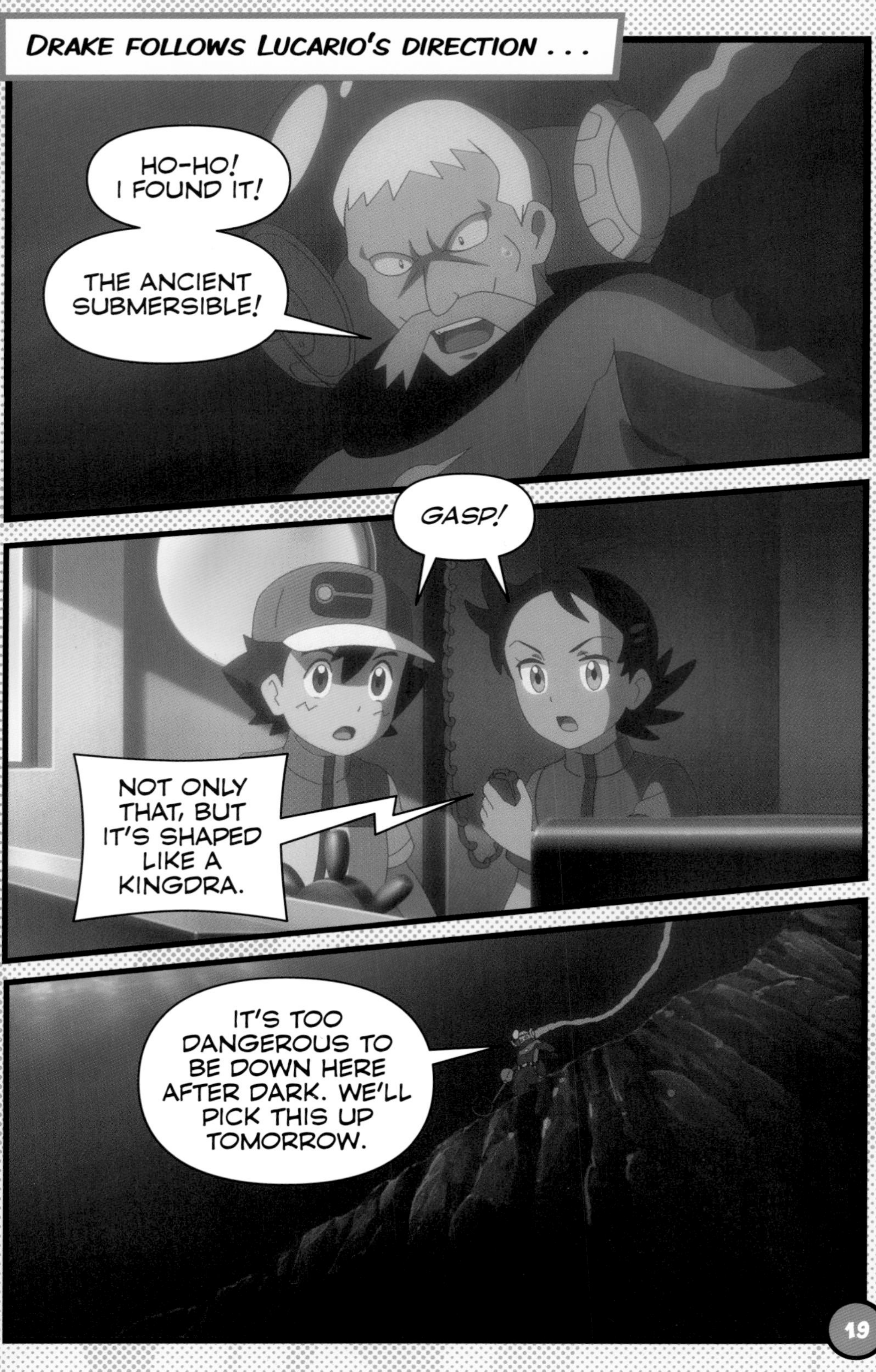
DRAKE FOLLOWS LUCARIO'S DIRECTION . . .
HO-HO! I FOUND IT!
THE ANCIENT SUBMERSIBLE!
GASP!
NOT ONLY THAT, BUT IT'S SHAPED LIKE A KINGDRA.
IT'S TOO DANGEROUS TO BE DOWN HERE AFTER DARK. WE'LL PICK THIS UP TOMORROW.

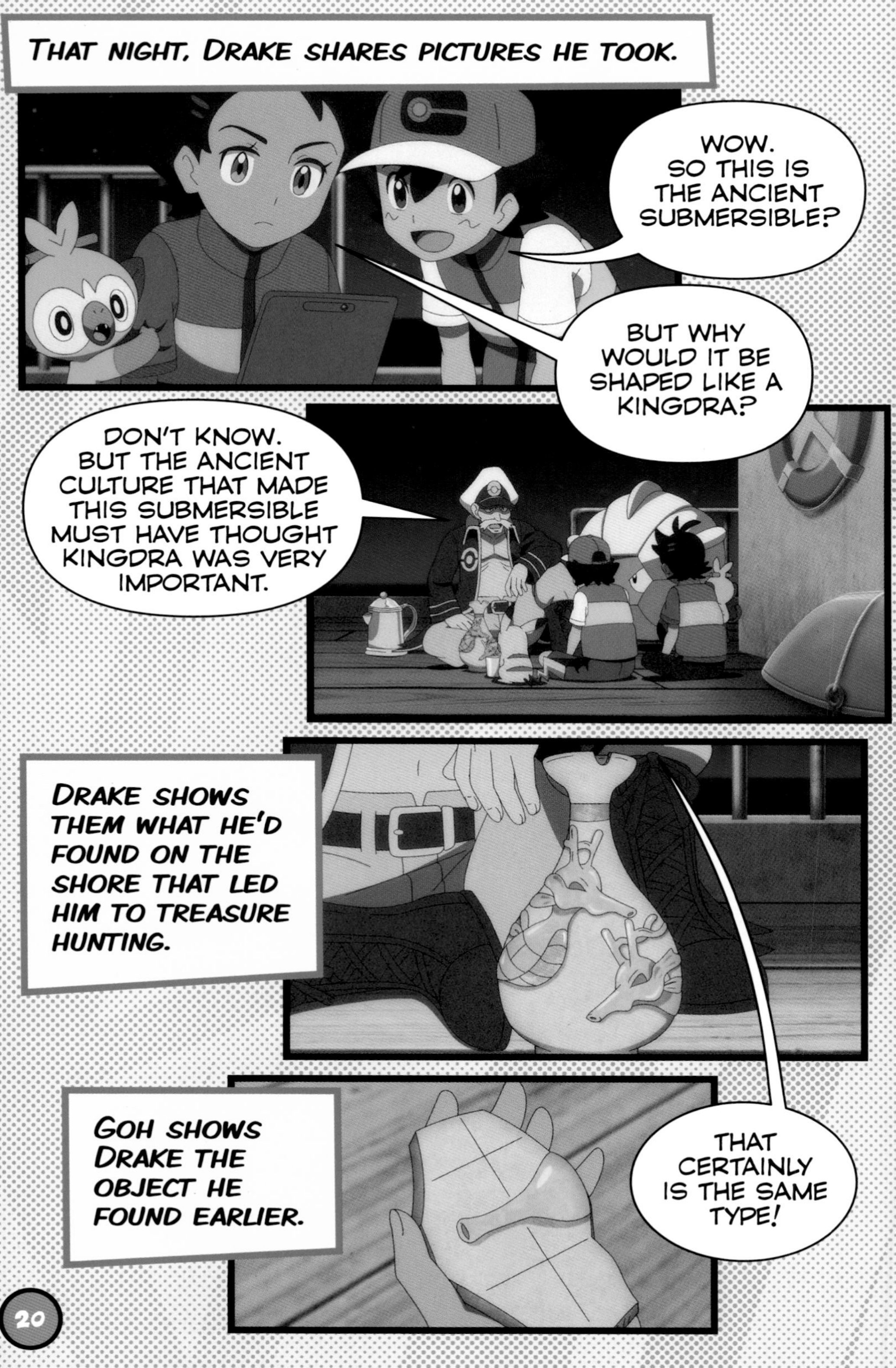

THAT NIGHT, DRAKE SHARES PICTURES HE TOOK.

WOW. SO THIS IS THE ANCIENT SUBMERSIBLE?

BUT WHY WOULD IT BE SHAPED LIKE A KINGDRA?

DON'T KNOW. BUT THE ANCIENT CULTURE THAT MADE THIS SUBMERSIBLE MUST HAVE THOUGHT KINGDRA WAS VERY IMPORTANT.

DRAKE SHOWS THEM WHAT HE'D FOUND ON THE SHORE THAT LED HIM TO TREASURE HUNTING.

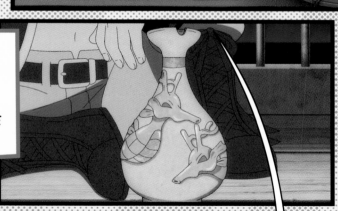

GOH SHOWS DRAKE THE OBJECT HE FOUND EARLIER.

THAT CERTAINLY IS THE SAME TYPE!

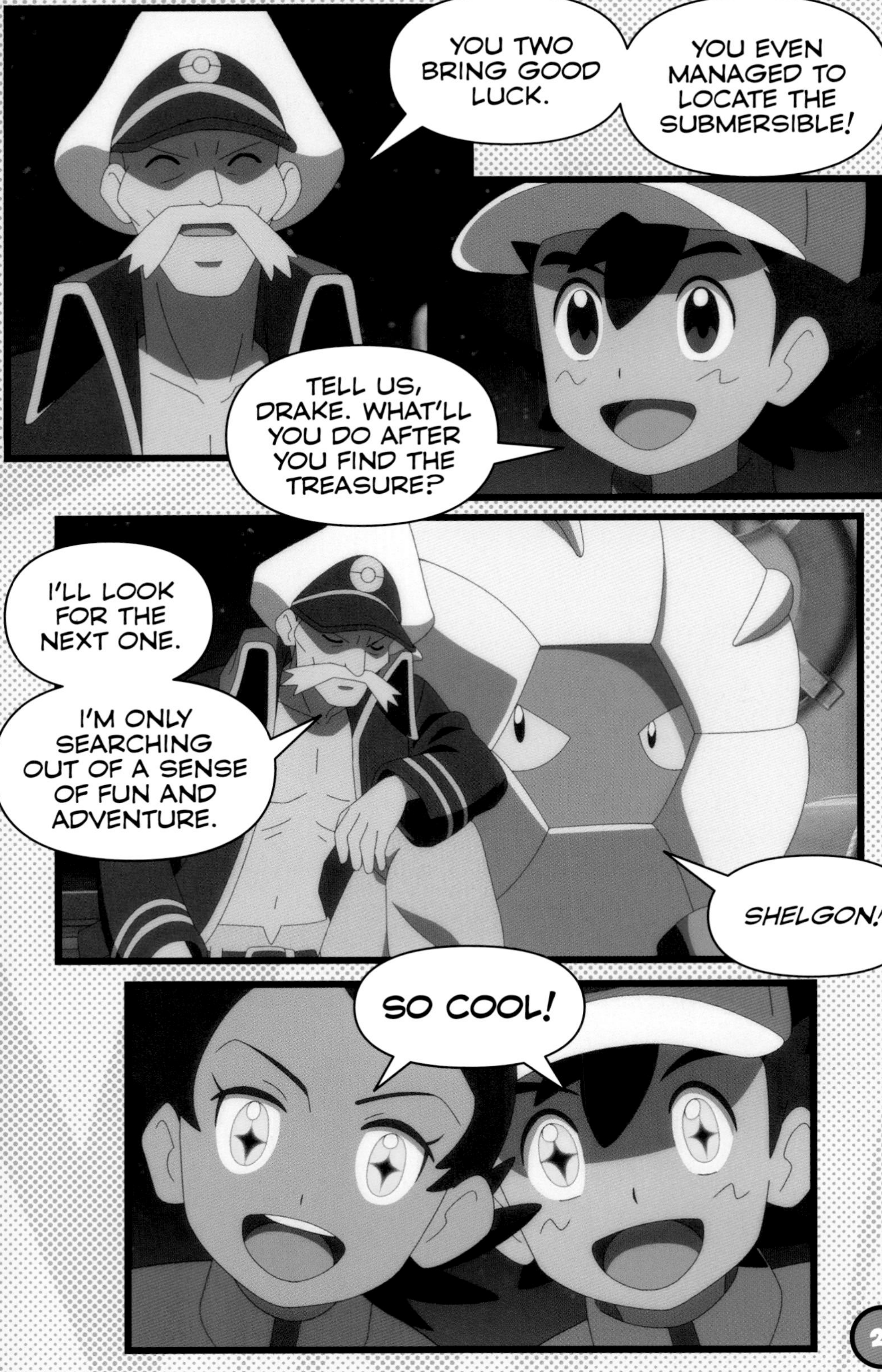
YOU TWO BRING GOOD LUCK.
YOU EVEN MANAGED TO LOCATE THE SUBMERSIBLE!
TELL US, DRAKE. WHAT'LL YOU DO AFTER YOU FIND THE TREASURE?
I'LL LOOK FOR THE NEXT ONE.
I'M ONLY SEARCHING OUT OF A SENSE OF FUN AND ADVENTURE.
SHELGON!
SO COOL!

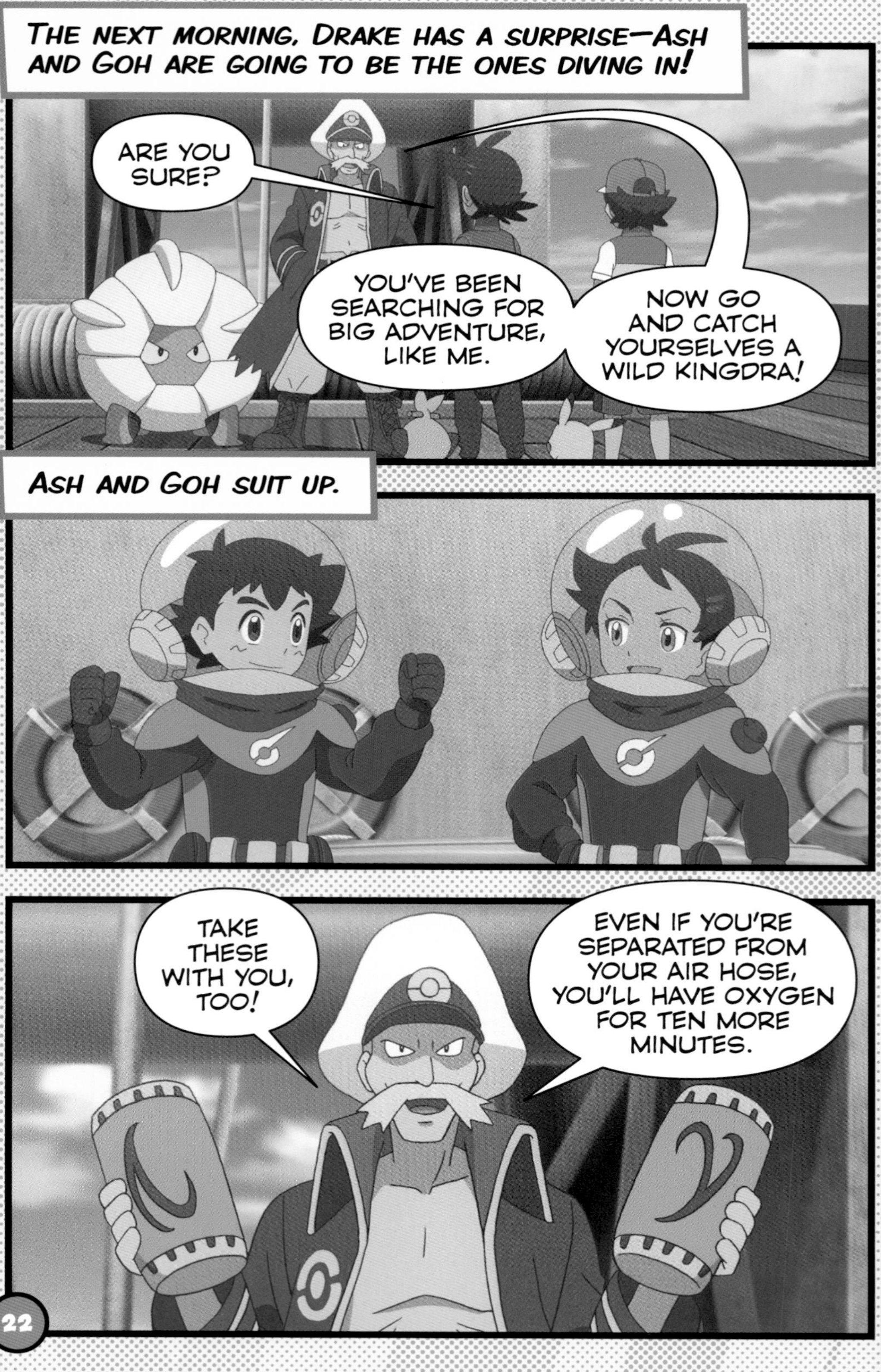
THE NEXT MORNING, DRAKE HAS A SURPRISE—ASH AND GOH ARE GOING TO BE THE ONES DIVING IN!
ARE YOU SURE?
YOU'VE BEEN SEARCHING FOR BIG ADVENTURE, LIKE ME.
NOW GO AND CATCH YOURSELVES A WILD KINGDRA!
ASH AND GOH SUIT UP.
TAKE THESE WITH YOU, TOO!
EVEN IF YOU'RE SEPARATED FROM YOUR AIR HOSE, YOU'LL HAVE OXYGEN FOR TEN MORE MINUTES.

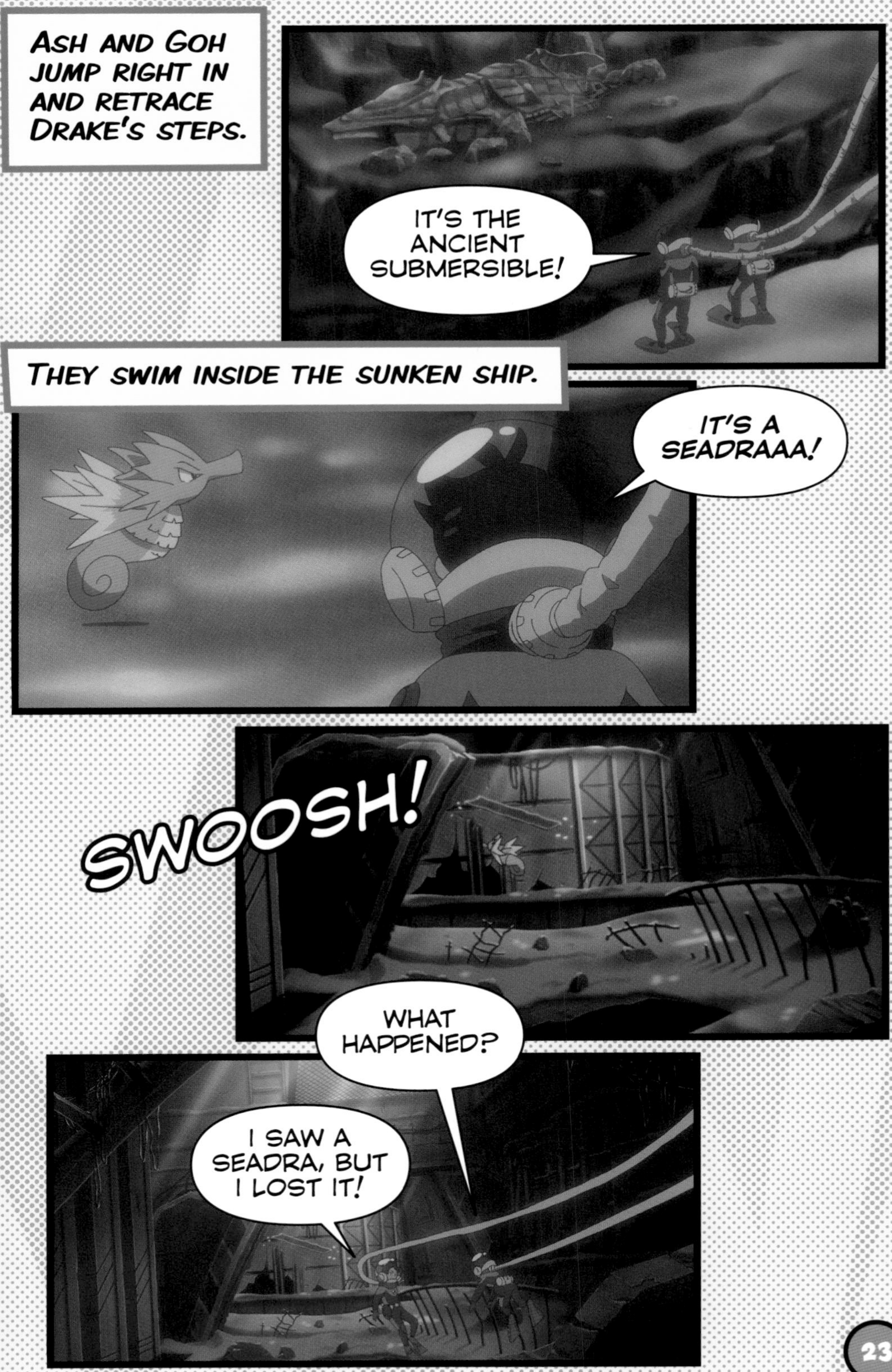
Ash and Goh jump right in and retrace Drake's steps.
It's the ancient submersible!
They swim inside the sunken ship.
It's a Seadraaa!
SWOOSH!
What happened?
I saw a Seadra, but I lost it!

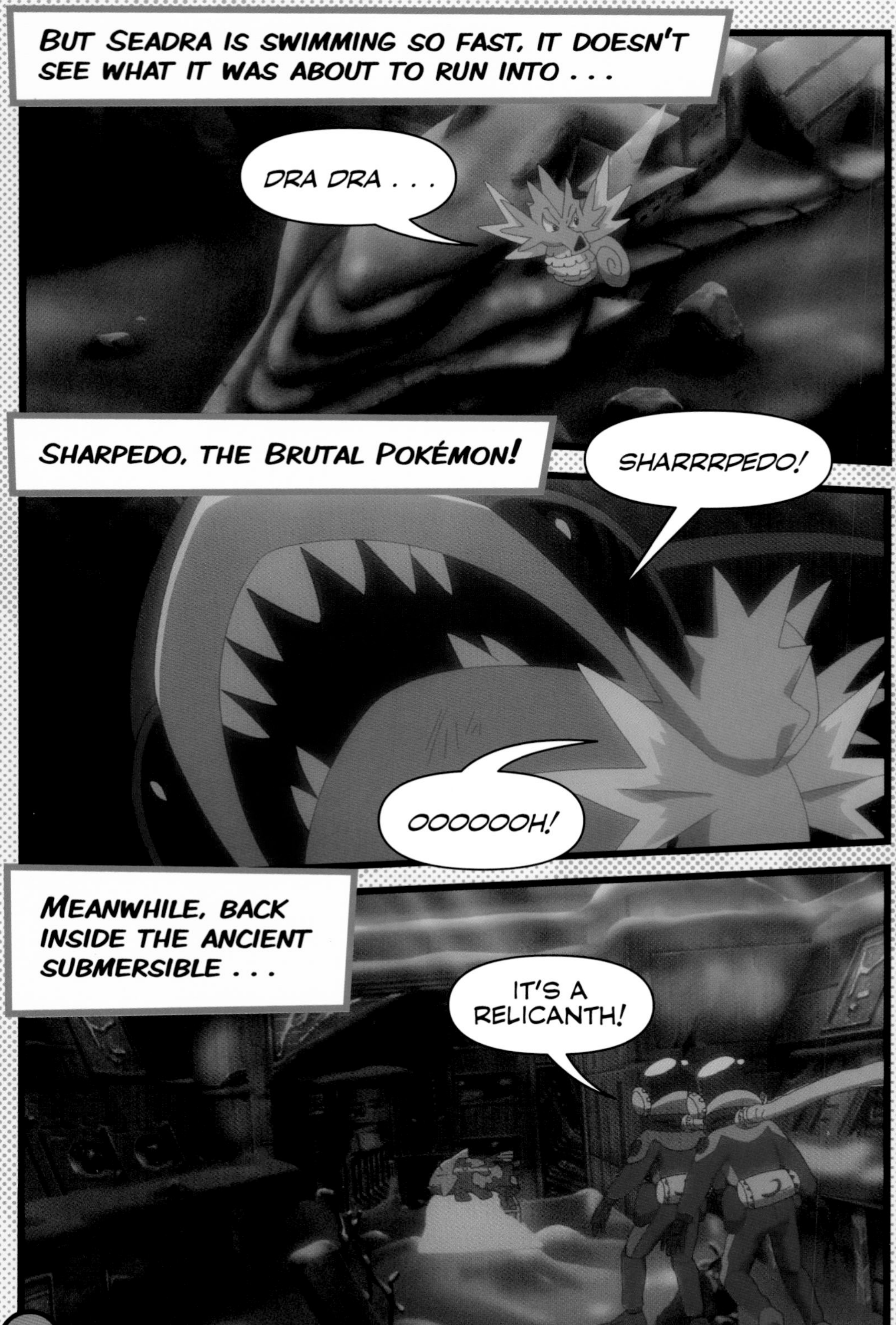
BUT SEADRA IS SWIMMING SO FAST, IT DOESN'T SEE WHAT IT WAS ABOUT TO RUN INTO . . .
DRA DRA . . .
SHARPEDO, THE BRUTAL POKÉMON!
SHARRRPEDO!
OOOOOOH!
MEANWHILE, BACK INSIDE THE ANCIENT SUBMERSIBLE . . .
IT'S A RELICANTH!

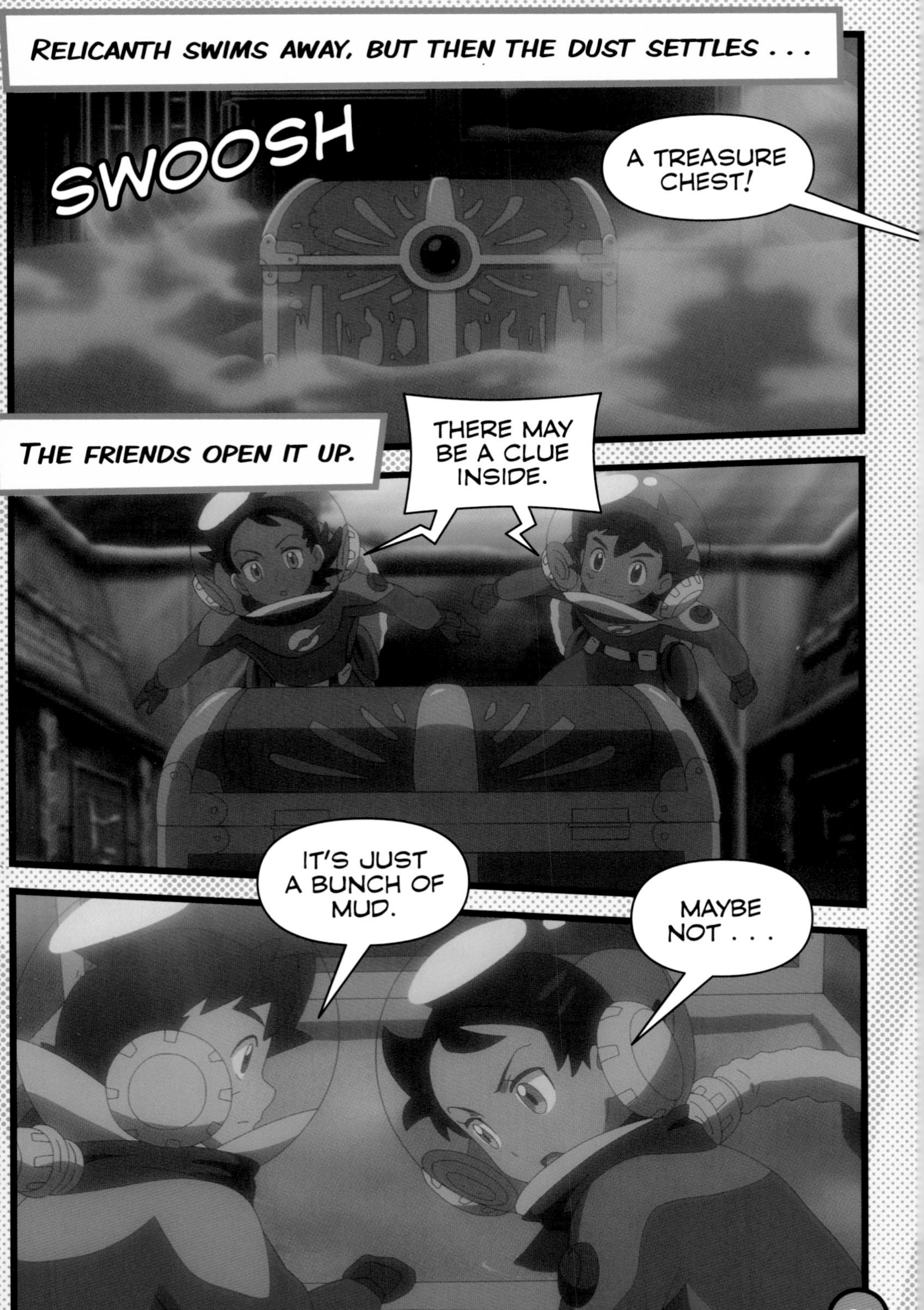
RELICANTH SWIMS AWAY, BUT THEN THE DUST SETTLES . . .
SWOOSH
A TREASURE CHEST!
THE FRIENDS OPEN IT UP.
THERE MAY BE A CLUE INSIDE.
IT'S JUST A BUNCH OF MUD.
MAYBE NOT . . .

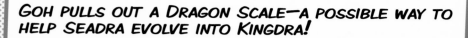

GOH PULLS OUT A DRAGON SCALE—A POSSIBLE WAY TO HELP SEADRA EVOLVE INTO KINGDRA!

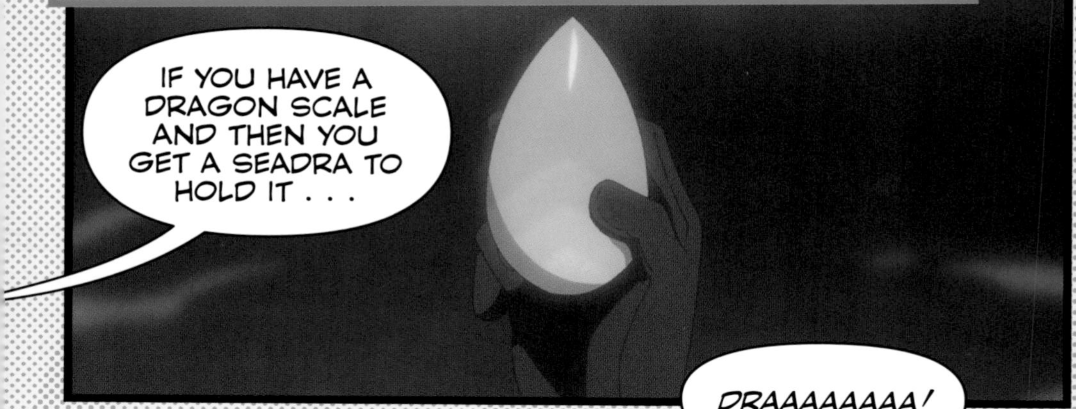
IF YOU HAVE A DRAGON SCALE AND THEN YOU GET A SEADRA TO HOLD IT . . .

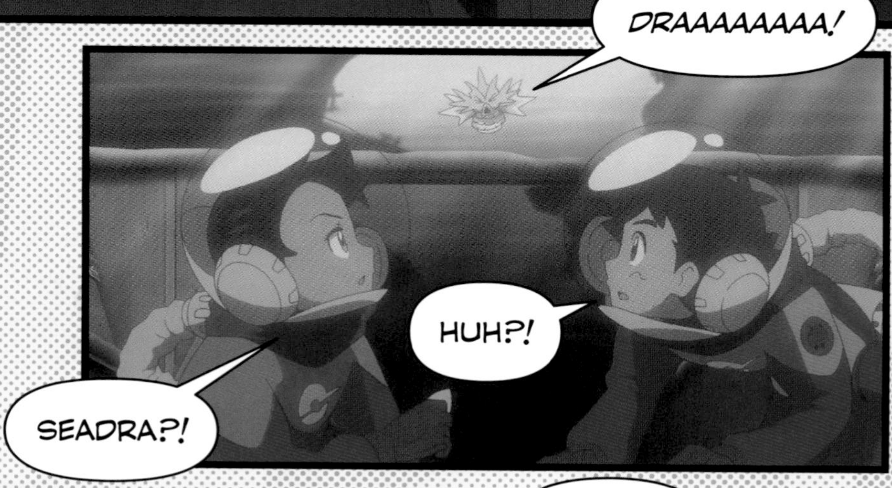
DRAAAAAAAA!
HUH?!
SEADRA?!

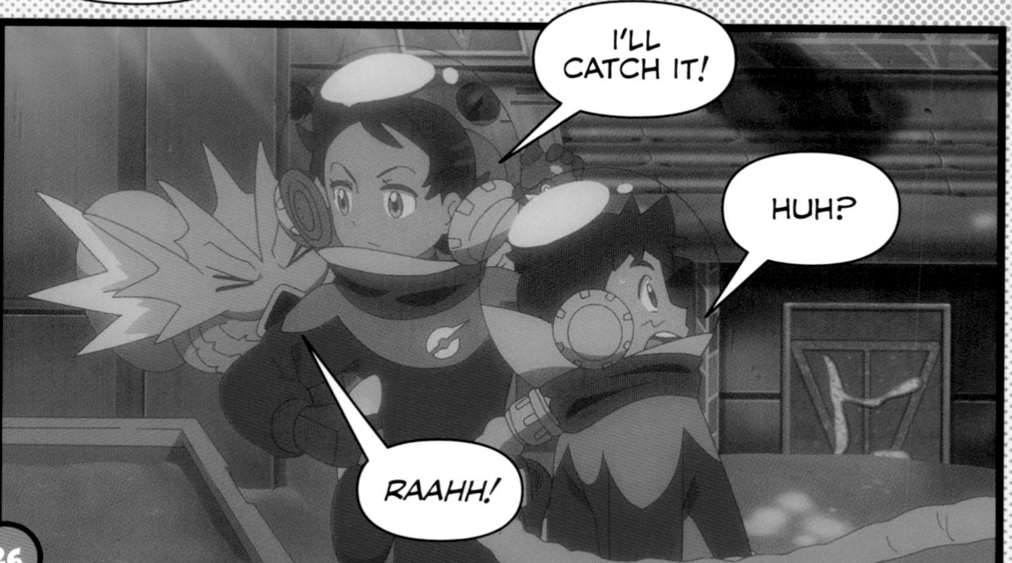
I'LL CATCH IT!
HUH?
RAAHH!

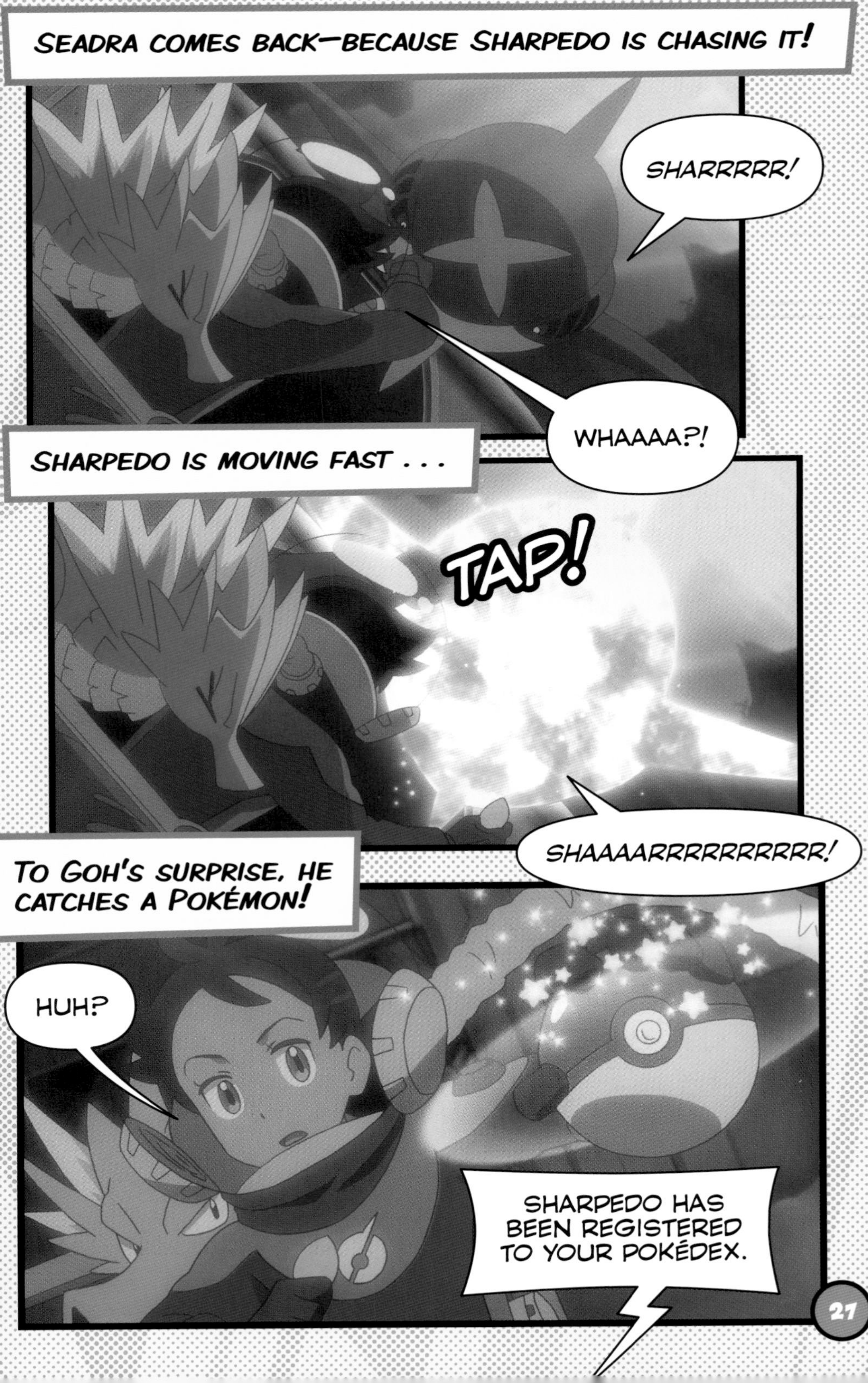

SEADRA COMES BACK—BECAUSE SHARPEDO IS CHASING IT!
SHARRRRR!
WHAAAA?!
SHARPEDO IS MOVING FAST . . .
TAP!
SHAAAARRRRRRRRR!
TO GOH'S SURPRISE, HE CATCHES A POKÉMON!
HUH?
SHARPEDO HAS BEEN REGISTERED TO YOUR POKÉDEX.

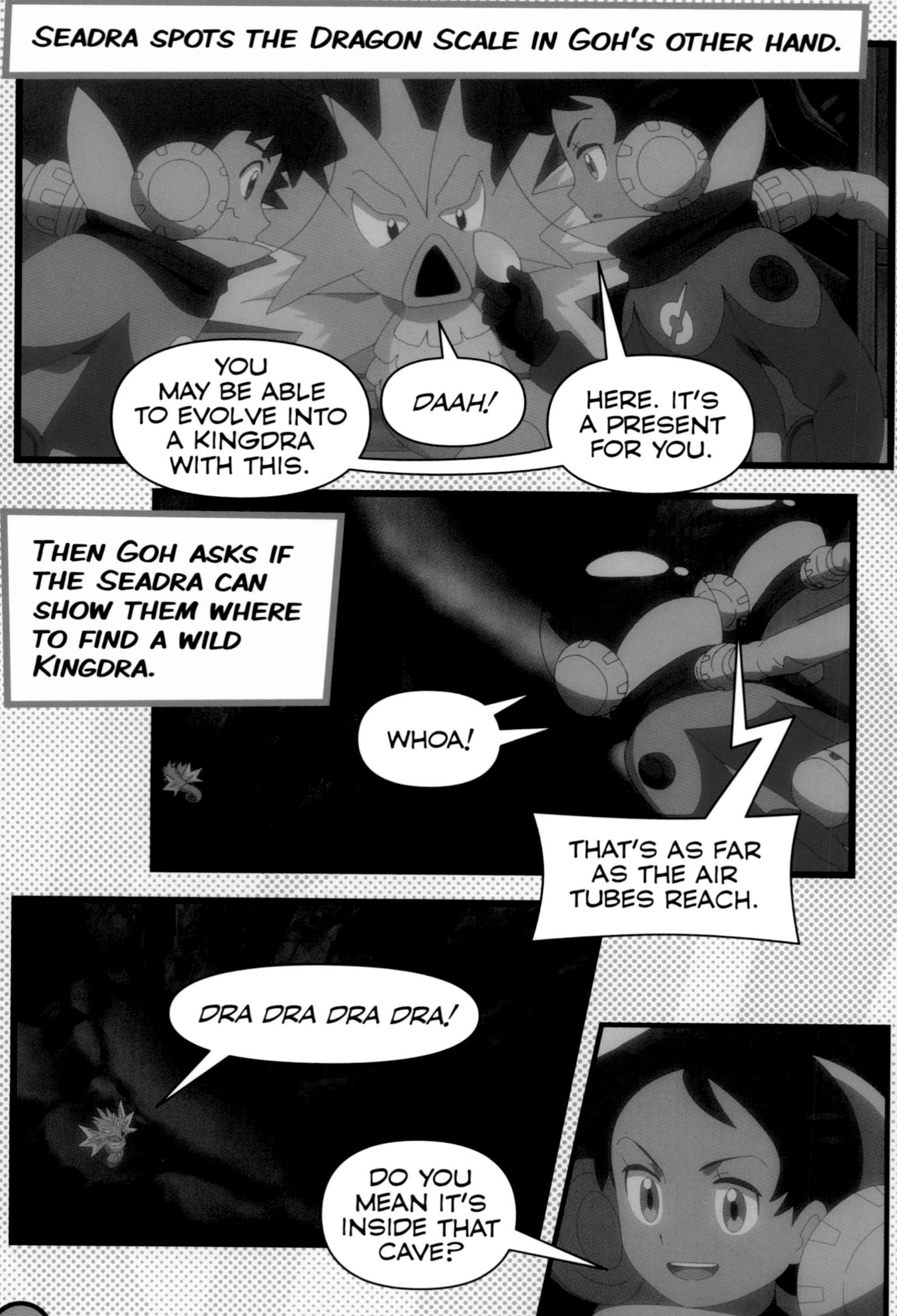
SEADRA SPOTS THE DRAGON SCALE IN GOH'S OTHER HAND.
YOU MAY BE ABLE TO EVOLVE INTO A KINGDRA WITH THIS.
DAAH!
HERE. IT'S A PRESENT FOR YOU.
THEN GOH ASKS IF THE SEADRA CAN SHOW THEM WHERE TO FIND A WILD KINGDRA.
WHOA!
THAT'S AS FAR AS THE AIR TUBES REACH.
DRA DRA DRA DRA!
DO YOU MEAN IT'S INSIDE THAT CAVE?

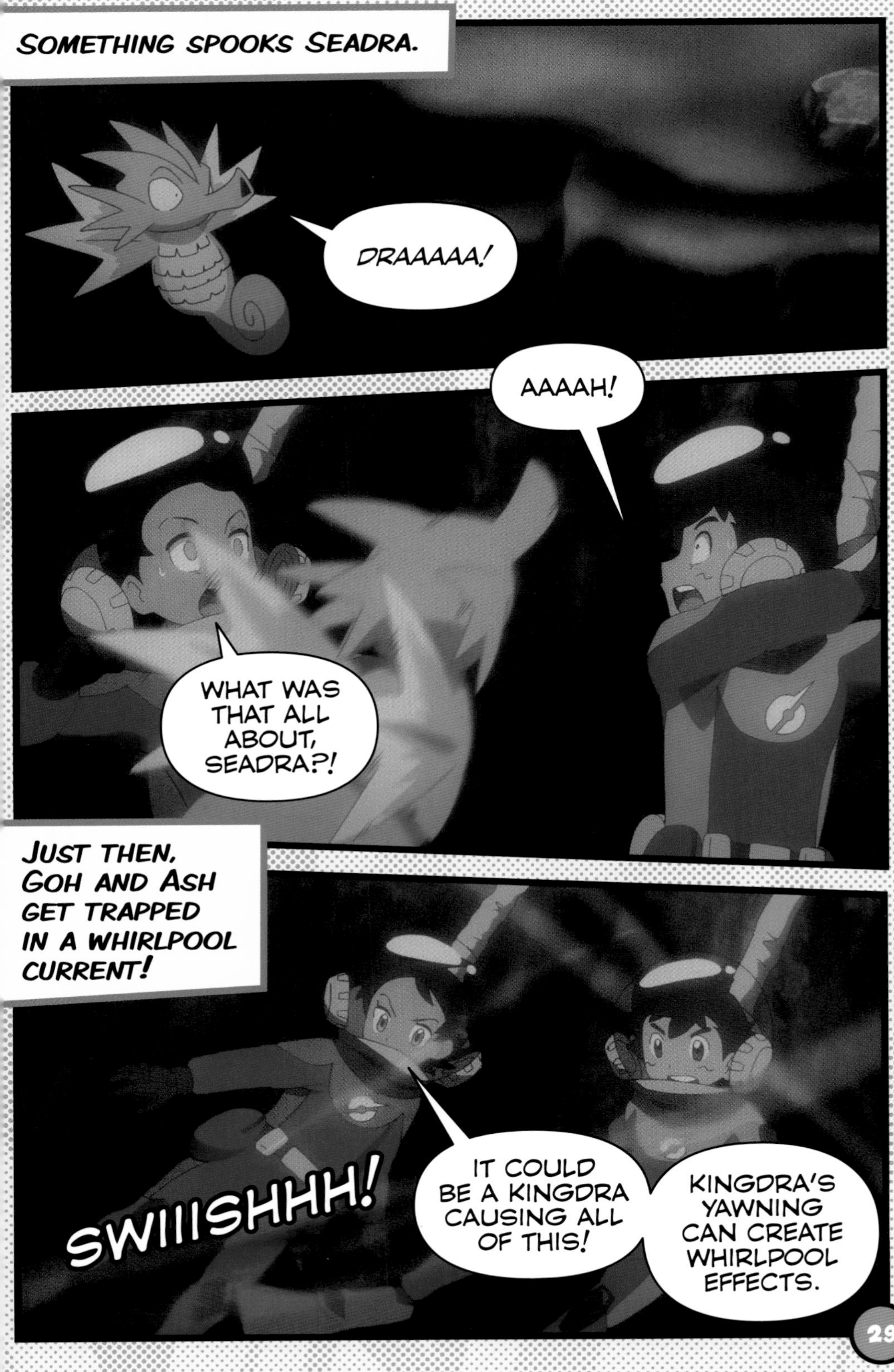
SOMETHING SPOOKS SEADRA.
DRAAAAA!
AAAAH!
WHAT WAS THAT ALL ABOUT, SEADRA?!
JUST THEN, GOH AND ASH GET TRAPPED IN A WHIRLPOOL CURRENT!
SWIIISHHH!
IT COULD BE A KINGDRA CAUSING ALL OF THIS!
KINGDRA'S YAWNING CAN CREATE WHIRLPOOL EFFECTS.

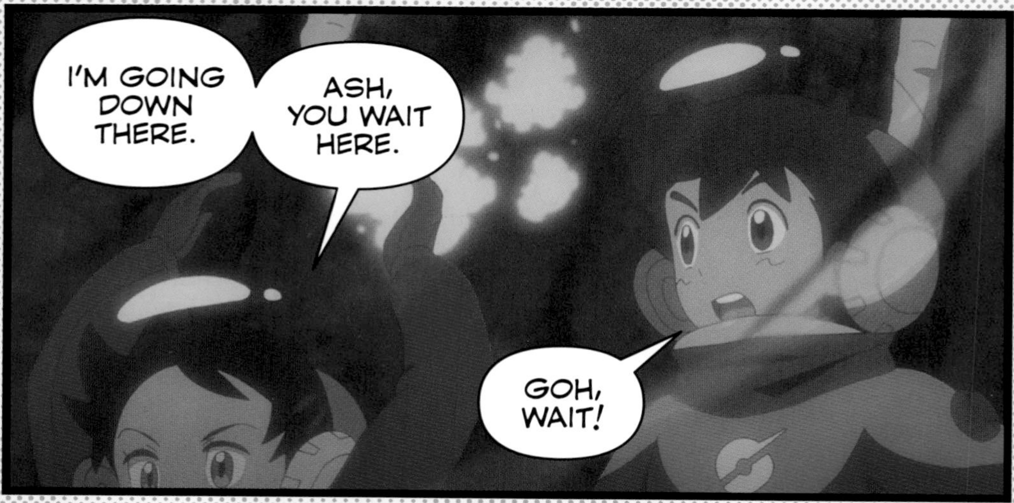
I'M GOING DOWN THERE.
ASH, YOU WAIT HERE.
GOH, WAIT!

GOH LETS THE WHIRLPOOL CARRY HIM DOWN . . .

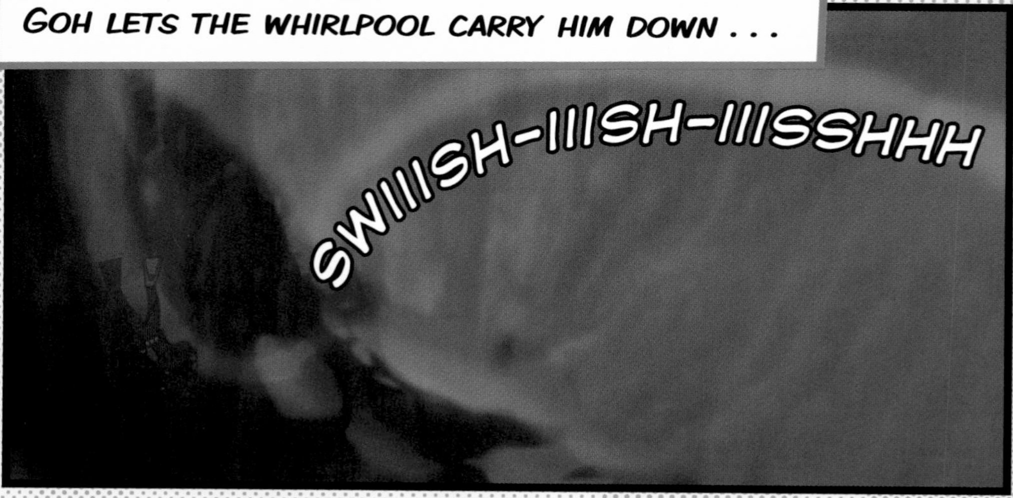
SWIIISH-IIISH-IIISSHHH

AND AROUND AND AROUND!

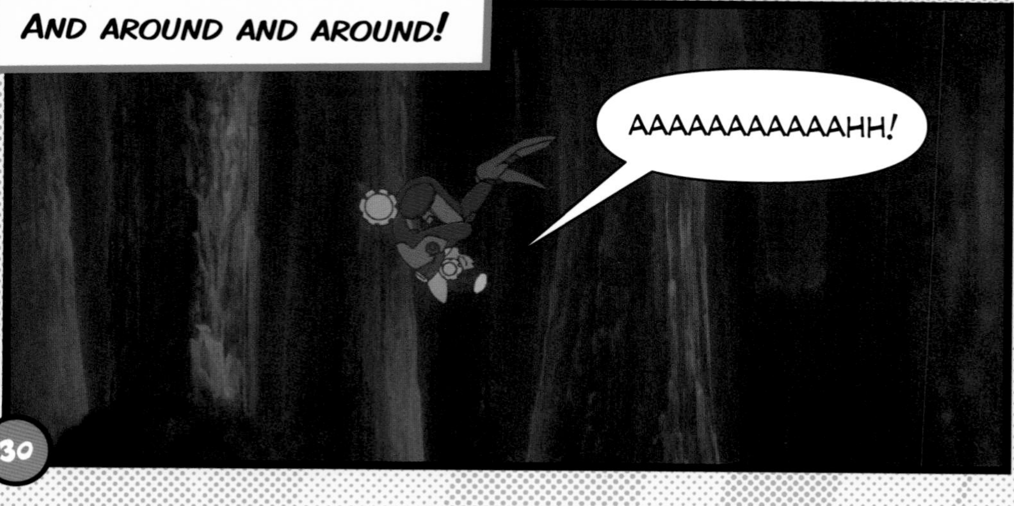
AAAAAAAAAAAAHH!

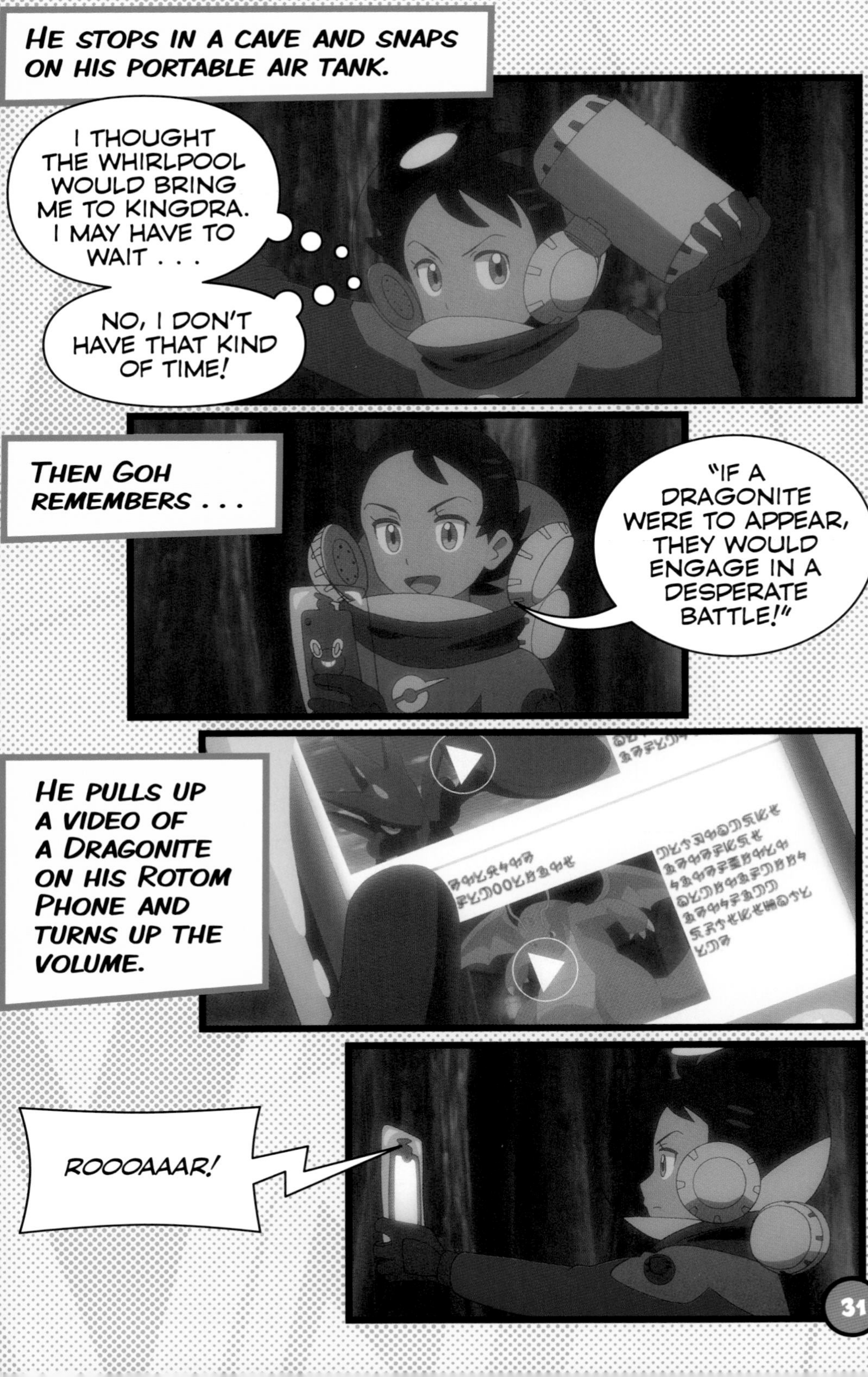

HE STOPS IN A CAVE AND SNAPS ON HIS PORTABLE AIR TANK.
I THOUGHT THE WHIRLPOOL WOULD BRING ME TO KINGDRA. I MAY HAVE TO WAIT . . .
NO, I DON'T HAVE THAT KIND OF TIME!
THEN GOH REMEMBERS . . .
"IF A DRAGONITE WERE TO APPEAR, THEY WOULD ENGAGE IN A DESPERATE BATTLE!"
HE PULLS UP A VIDEO OF A DRAGONITE ON HIS ROTOM PHONE AND TURNS UP THE VOLUME.
ROOOAAAR!

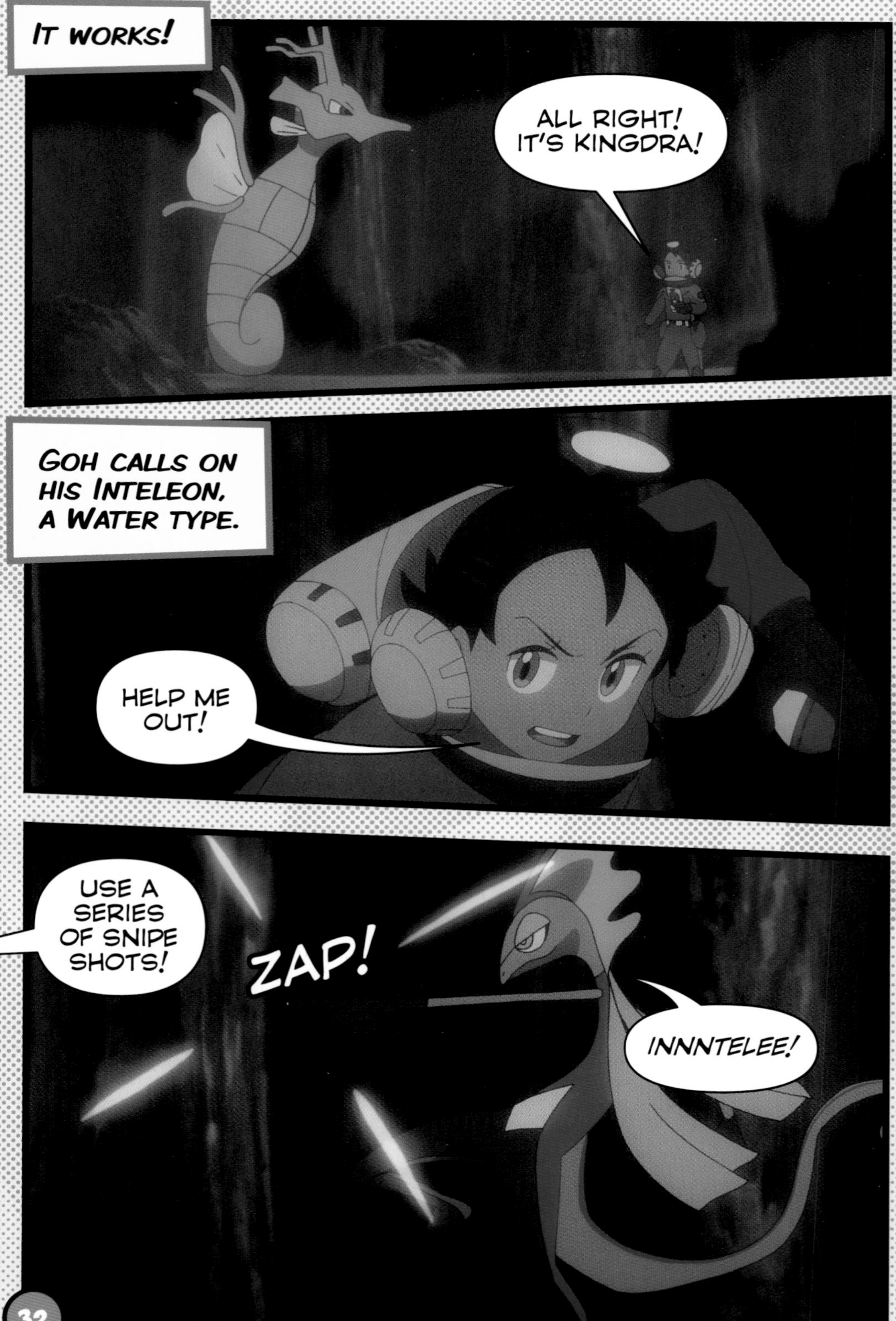
IT WORKS!
ALL RIGHT! IT'S KINGDRA!
GOH CALLS ON HIS INTELEON, A WATER TYPE.
HELP ME OUT!
USE A SERIES OF SNIPE SHOTS!
ZAP!
INNNTELEE!

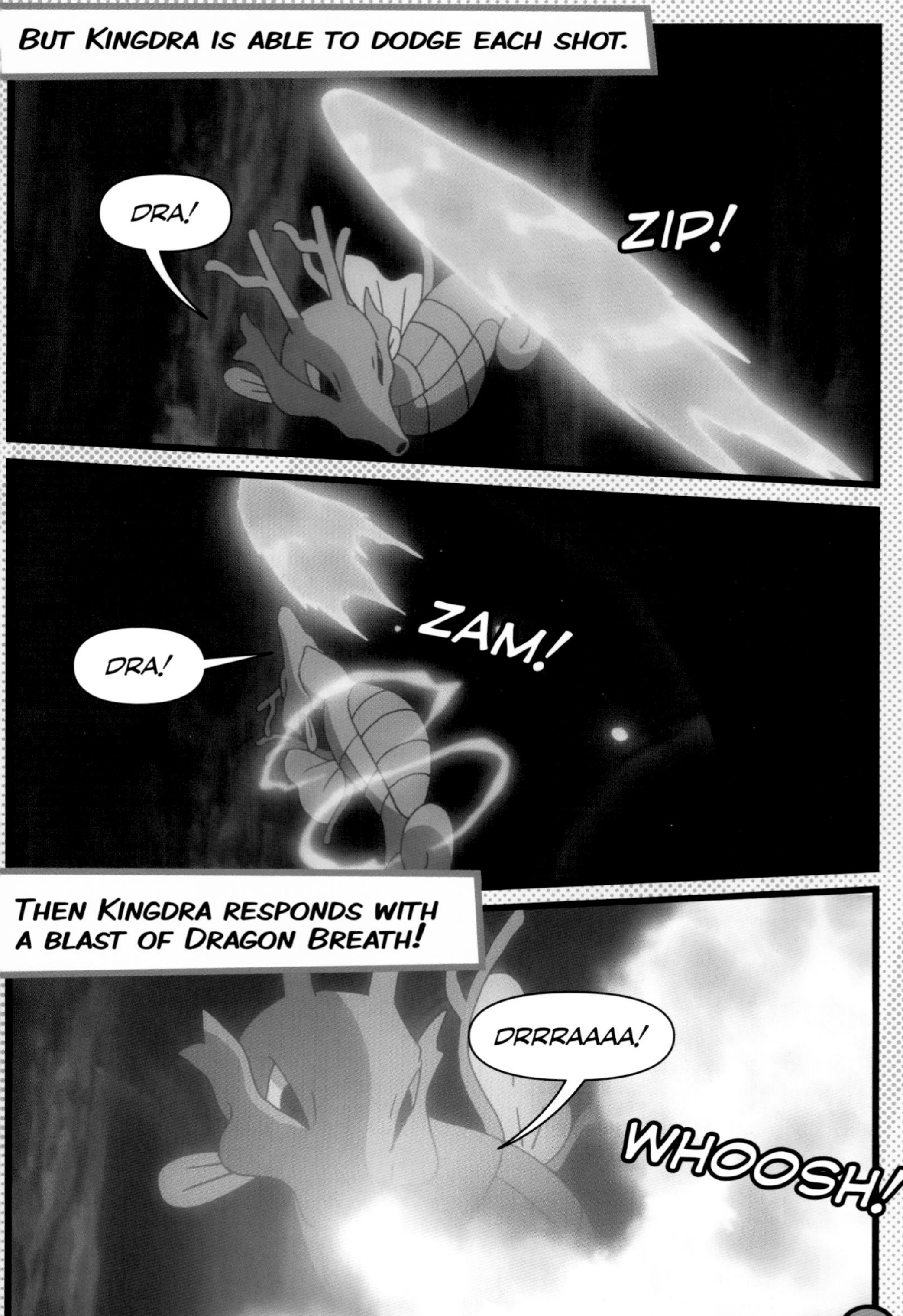
But Kingdra is able to dodge each shot.
DRA!
ZIP!
DRA!
ZAM!
Then Kingdra responds with a blast of Dragon Breath!
DRRRAAAA!
WHOOSH!

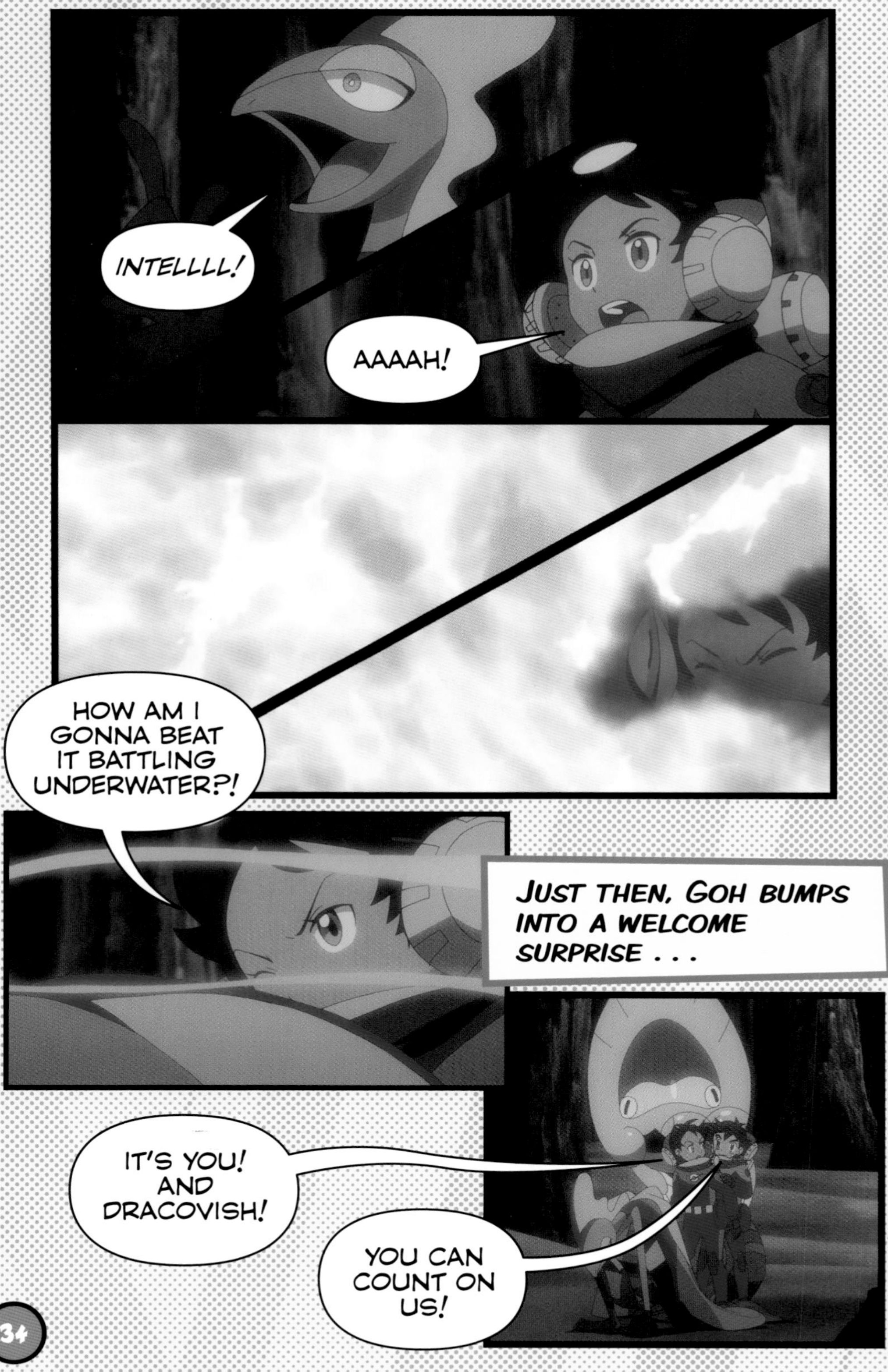
INTELLLL!
AAAAH!
HOW AM I GONNA BEAT IT BATTLING UNDERWATER?!
JUST THEN, GOH BUMPS INTO A WELCOME SURPRISE . . .
IT'S YOU! AND DRACOVISH!
YOU CAN COUNT ON US!

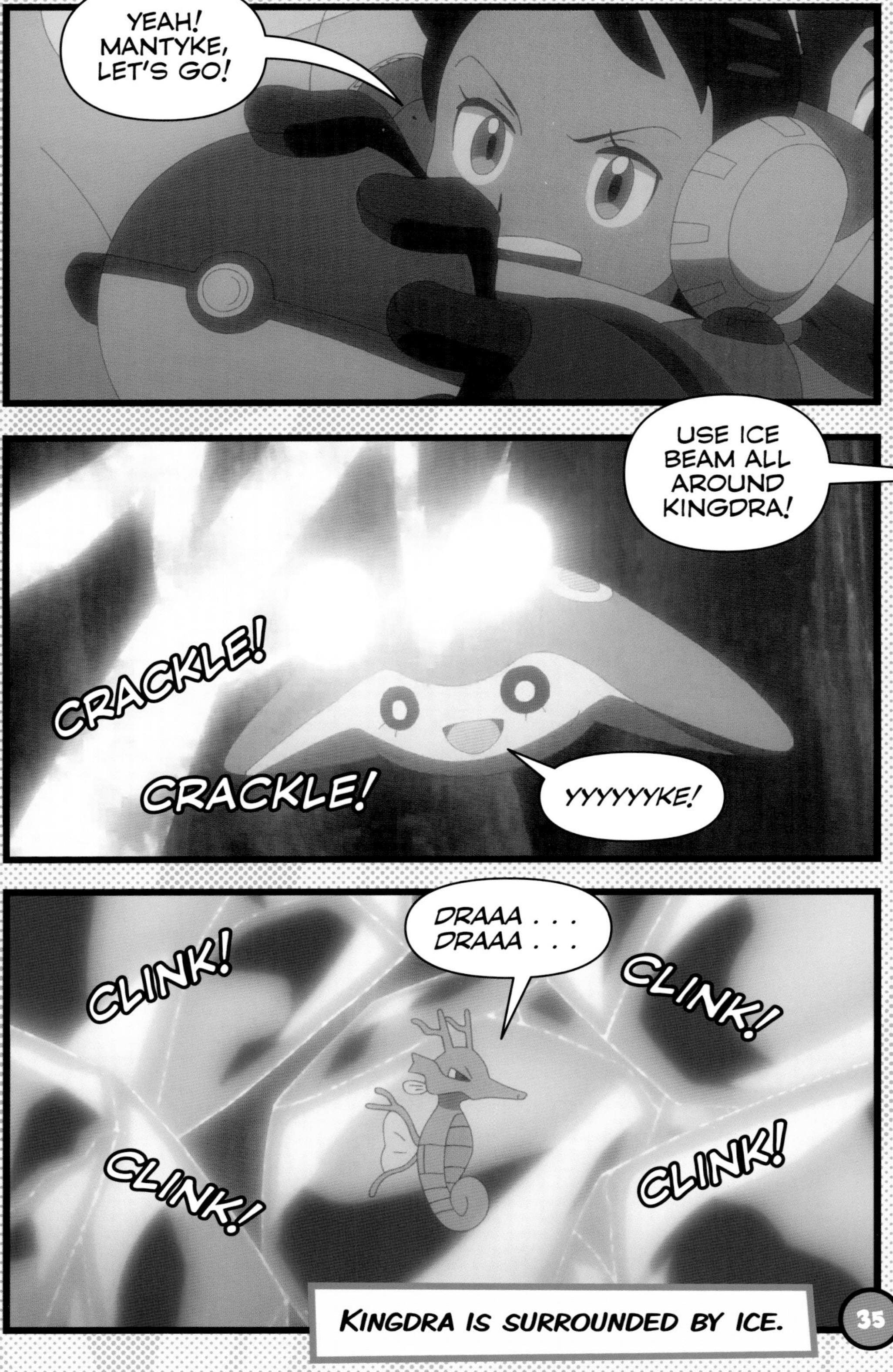
YEAH! MANTYKE, LET'S GO!
USE ICE BEAM ALL AROUND KINGDRA!
CRACKLE!
CRACKLE!
YYYYYYKE!
DRAAA . . . DRAAA . . .
CLINK!
CLINK!
CLINK!
CLINK!
KINGDRA IS SURROUNDED BY ICE.

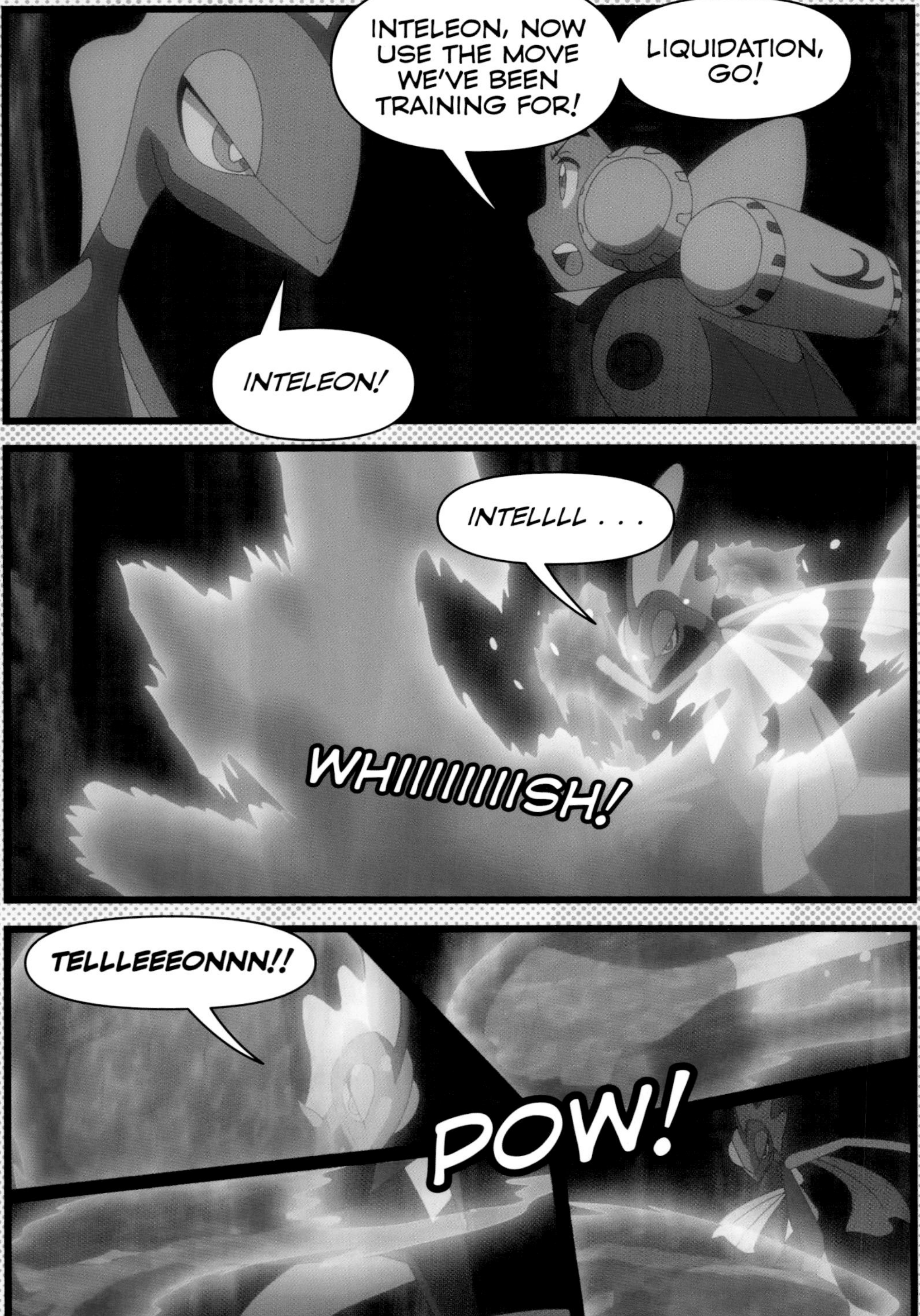
INTELEON, NOW USE THE MOVE WE'VE BEEN TRAINING FOR!
LIQUIDATION, GO!
INTELEON!
INTELLLL . . .
WHIIIIIIIIISH!
TELLLEEEONNN!!
POW!

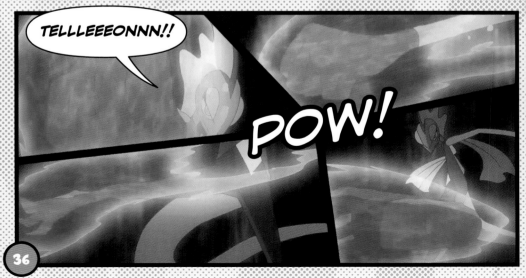

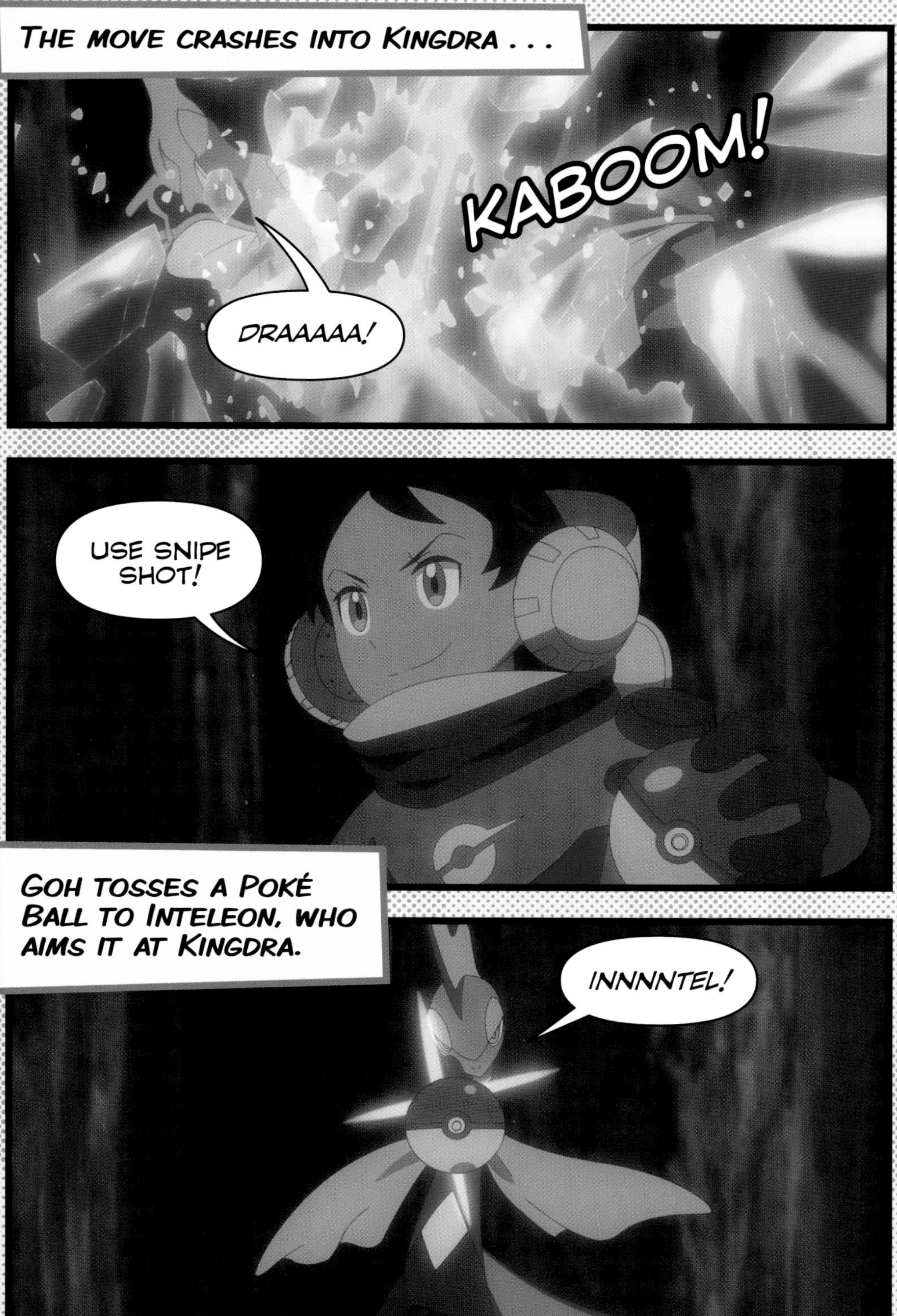
THE MOVE CRASHES INTO KINGDRA . . .
KABOOM!
DRAAAAA!
USE SNIPE SHOT!
GOH TOSSES A POKÉ BALL TO INTELEON, WHO AIMS IT AT KINGDRA.
INNNNTEL!

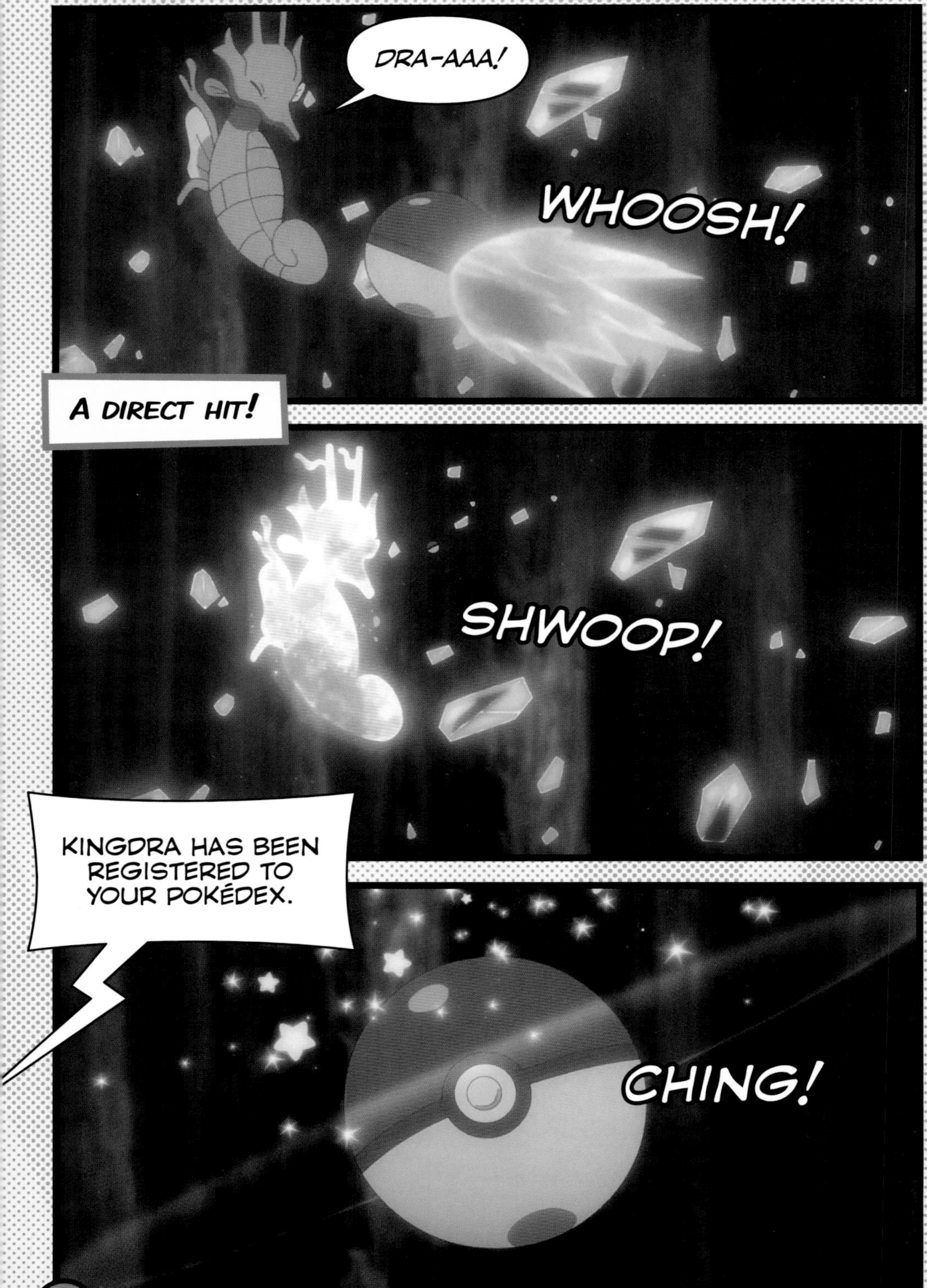
DRA-AAA!
WHOOSH!
A DIRECT HIT!
SHWOOP!
KINGDRA HAS BEEN REGISTERED TO YOUR POKÉDEX.
CHING!

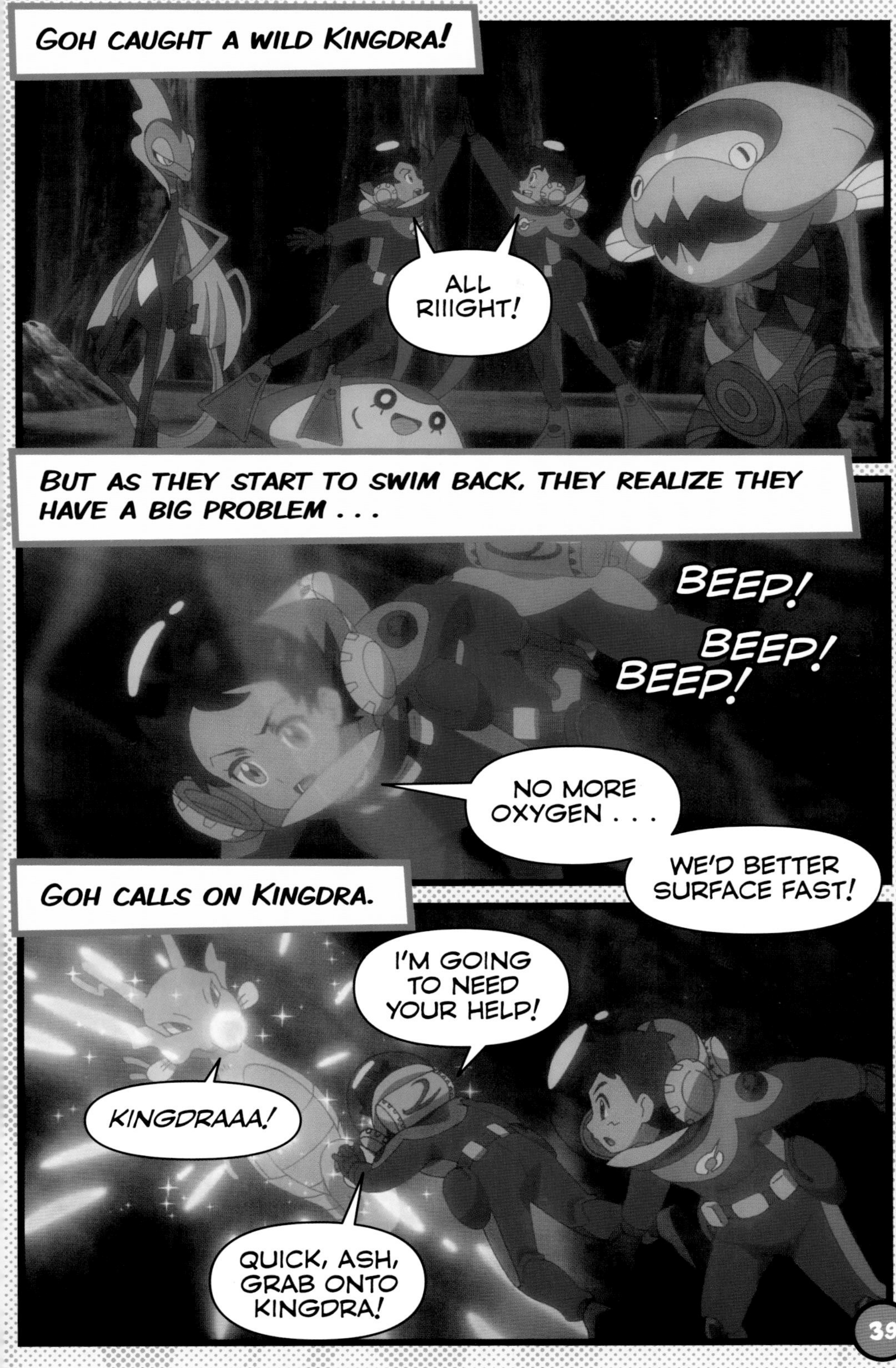
GOH CAUGHT A WILD KINGDRA!
ALL RIIIGHT!
BUT AS THEY START TO SWIM BACK, THEY REALIZE THEY HAVE A BIG PROBLEM . . .
BEEP! BEEP! BEEP!
NO MORE OXYGEN . . .
WE'D BETTER SURFACE FAST!
GOH CALLS ON KINGDRA.
I'M GOING TO NEED YOUR HELP!
KINGDRAAA!
QUICK, ASH, GRAB ONTO KINGDRA!

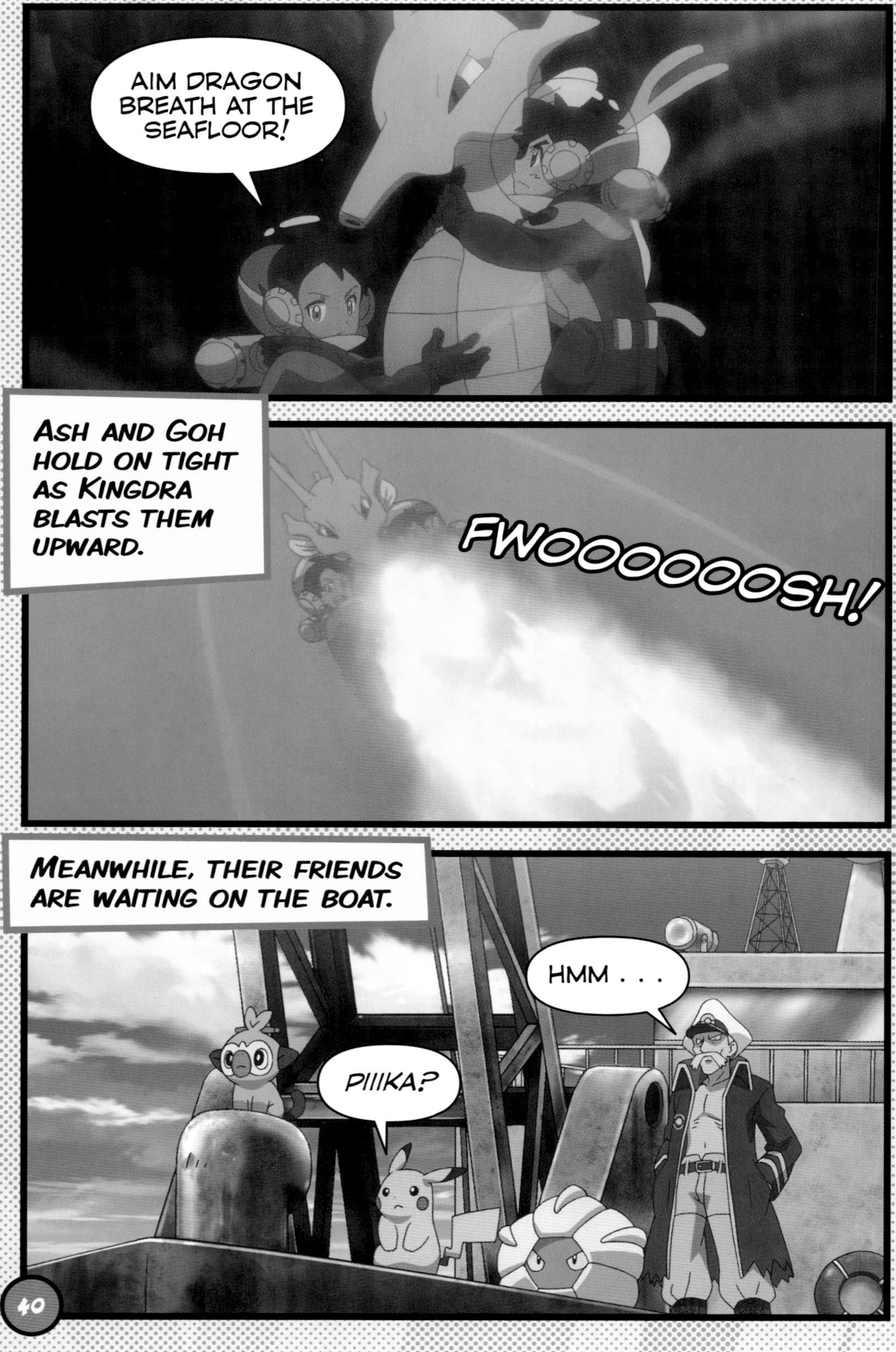
AIM DRAGON BREATH AT THE SEAFLOOR!
ASH AND GOH HOLD ON TIGHT AS KINGDRA BLASTS THEM UPWARD.
FWOOOOOOOSH!
MEANWHILE, THEIR FRIENDS ARE WAITING ON THE BOAT.
HMM . . .
PIIIKA?

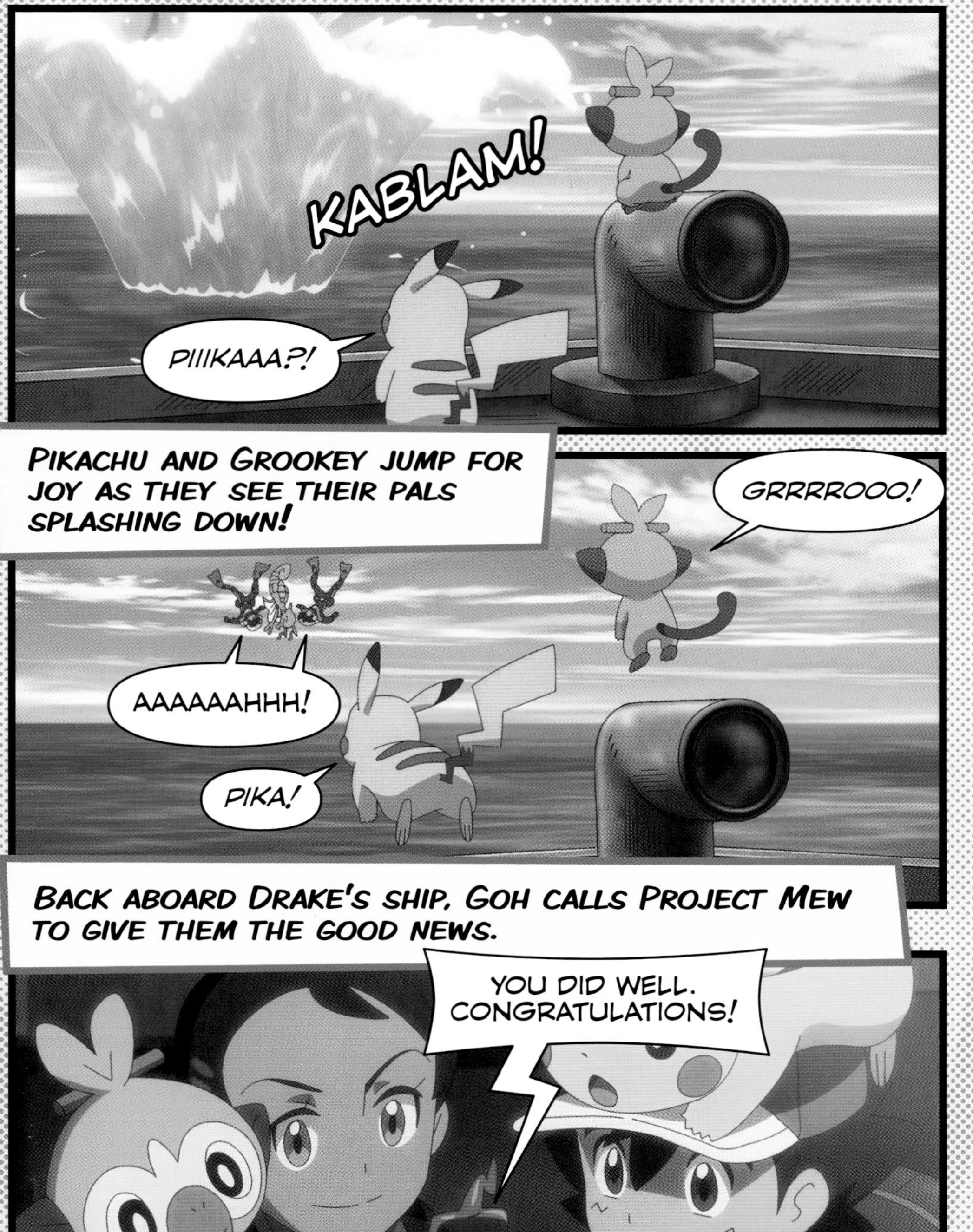
KABLAM!
PIIIKAAA?!
PIKACHU AND GROOKEY JUMP FOR JOY AS THEY SEE THEIR PALS SPLASHING DOWN!
GRRRROOO!
AAAAAAHHH!
PIKA!
BACK ABOARD DRAKE'S SHIP, GOH CALLS PROJECT MEW TO GIVE THEM THE GOOD NEWS.
YOU DID WELL. CONGRATULATIONS!
THANK YOU SO MUCH!

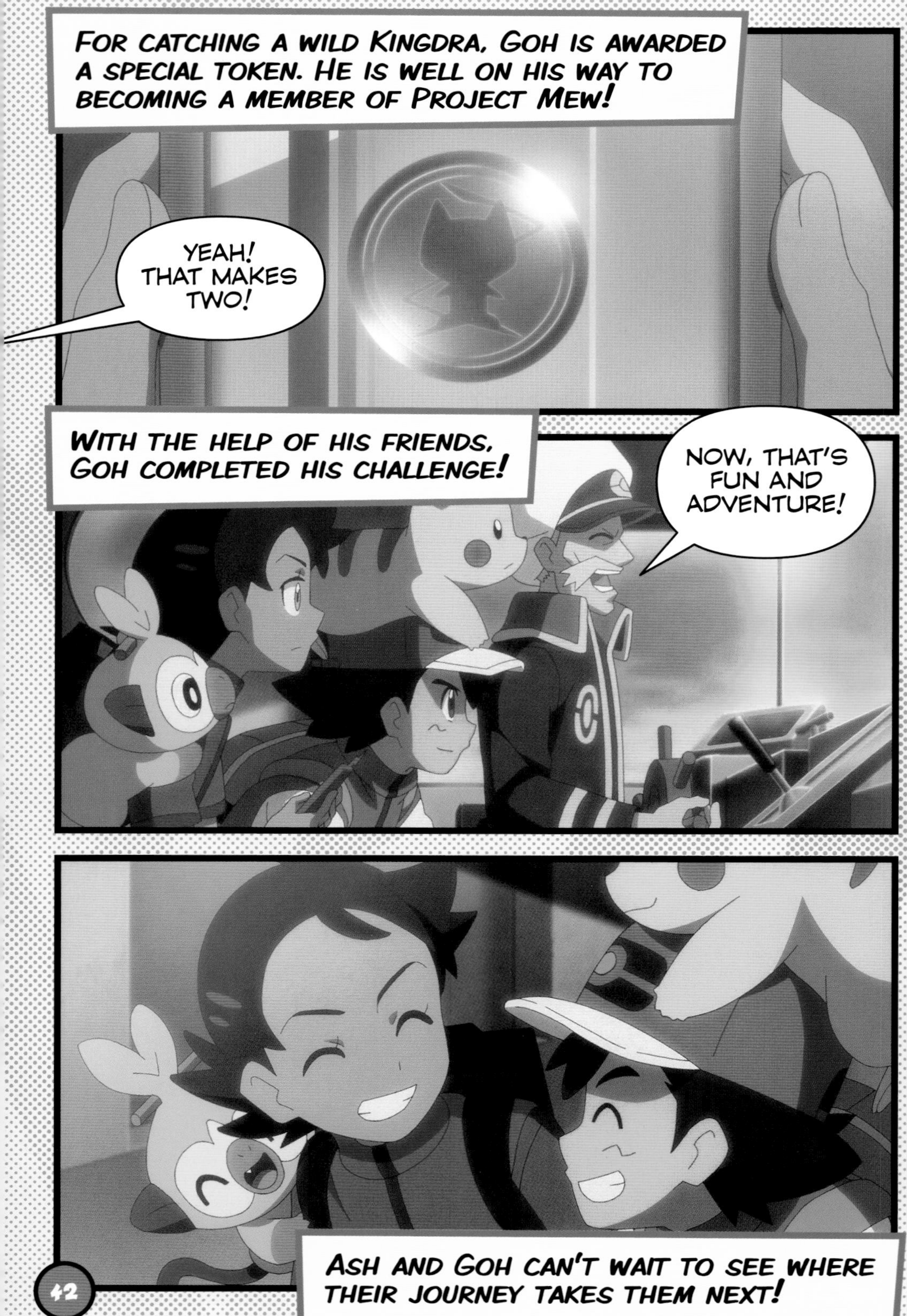
FOR CATCHING A WILD KINGDRA, GOH IS AWARDED A SPECIAL TOKEN. HE IS WELL ON HIS WAY TO BECOMING A MEMBER OF PROJECT MEW!
YEAH! THAT MAKES TWO!
WITH THE HELP OF HIS FRIENDS, GOH COMPLETED HIS CHALLENGE!
NOW, THAT'S FUN AND ADVENTURE!
ASH AND GOH CAN'T WAIT TO SEE WHERE THEIR JOURNEY TAKES THEM NEXT!

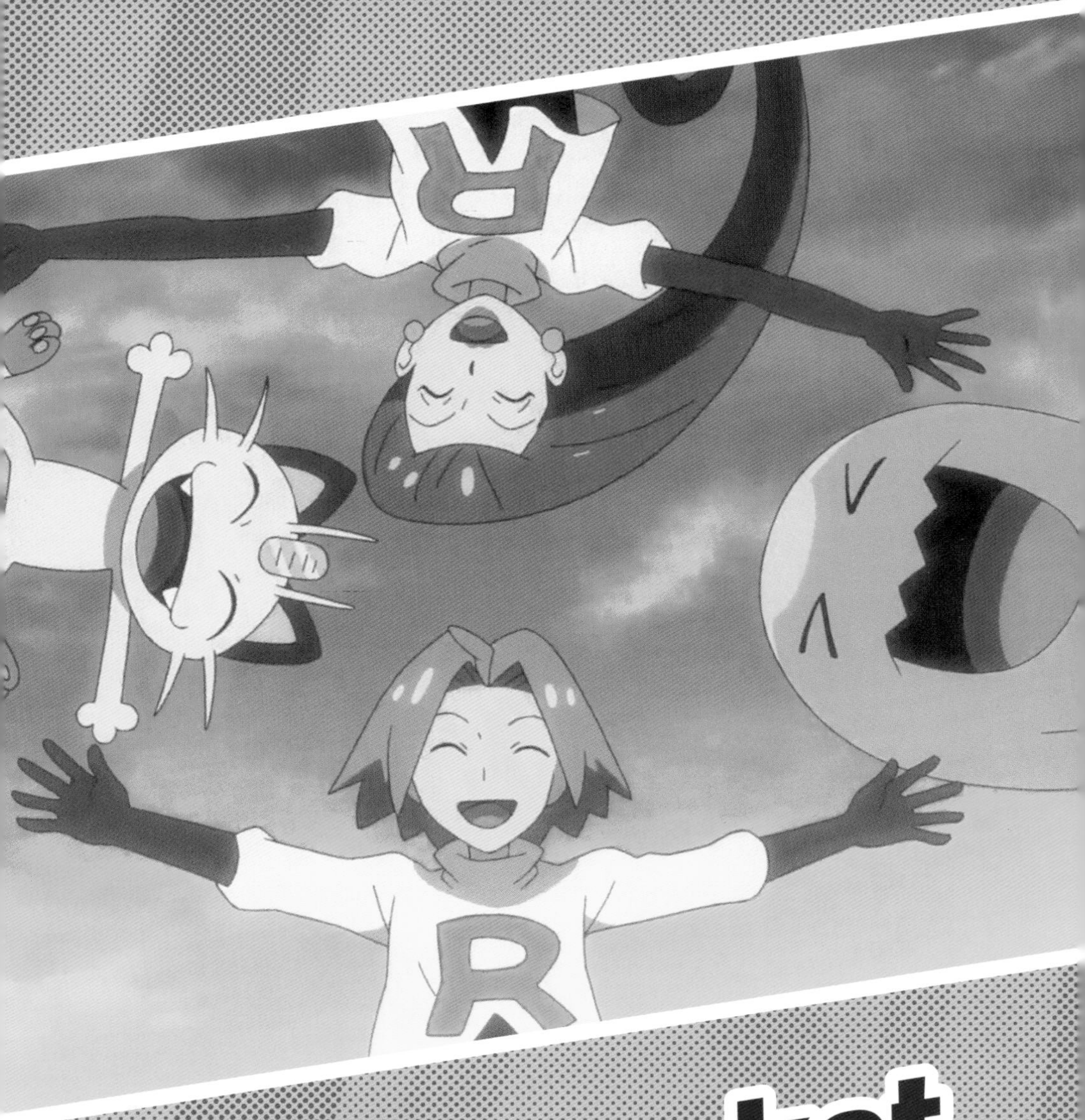

Team Rocket in Luck

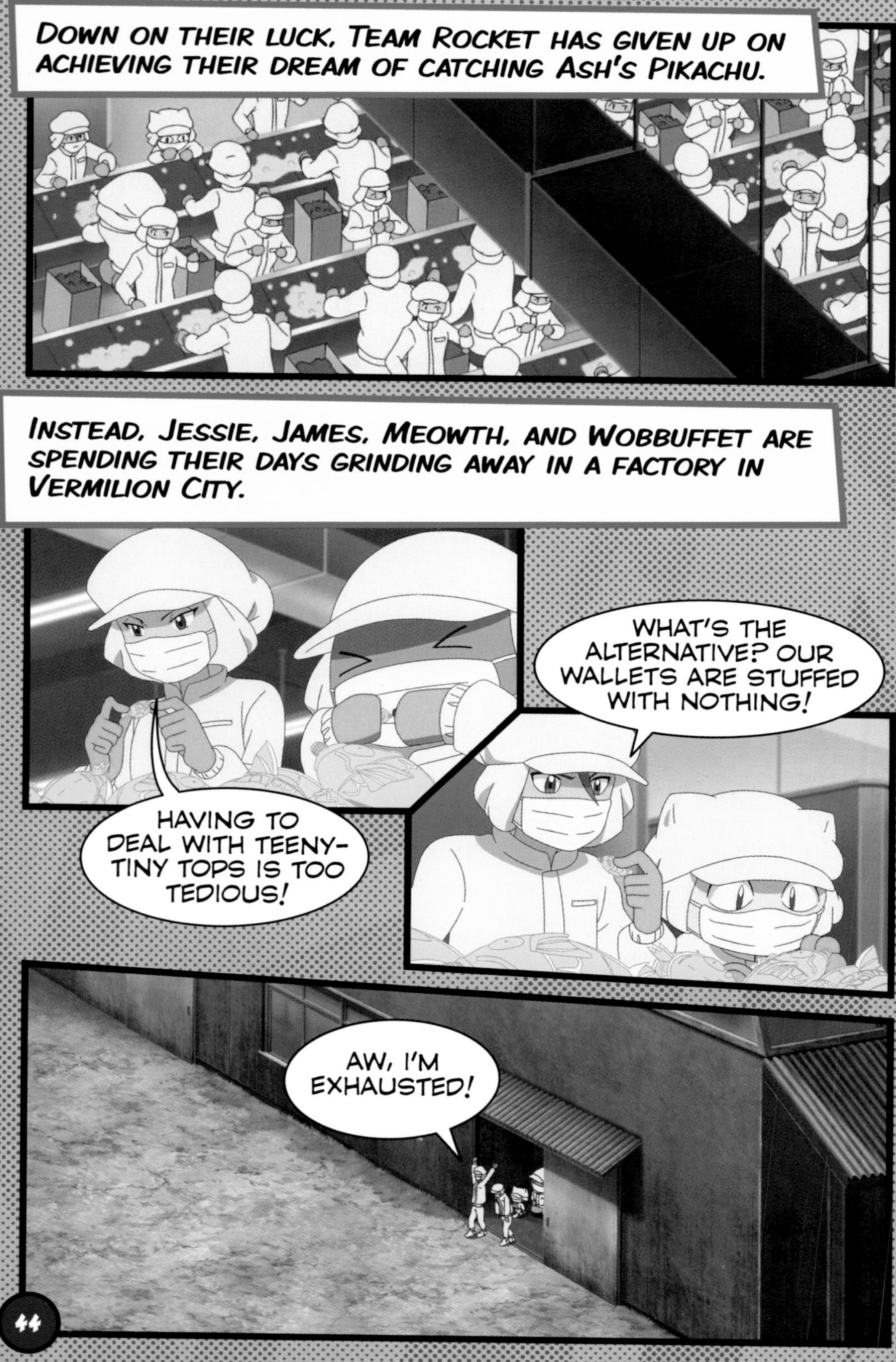
DOWN ON THEIR LUCK, TEAM ROCKET HAS GIVEN UP ON ACHIEVING THEIR DREAM OF CATCHING ASH'S PIKACHU.
INSTEAD, JESSIE, JAMES, MEOWTH, AND WOBBUFFET ARE SPENDING THEIR DAYS GRINDING AWAY IN A FACTORY IN VERMILION CITY.
HAVING TO DEAL WITH TEENY-TINY TOPS IS TOO TEDIOUS!
WHAT'S THE ALTERNATIVE? OUR WALLETS ARE STUFFED WITH NOTHING!
AW, I'M EXHAUSTED!

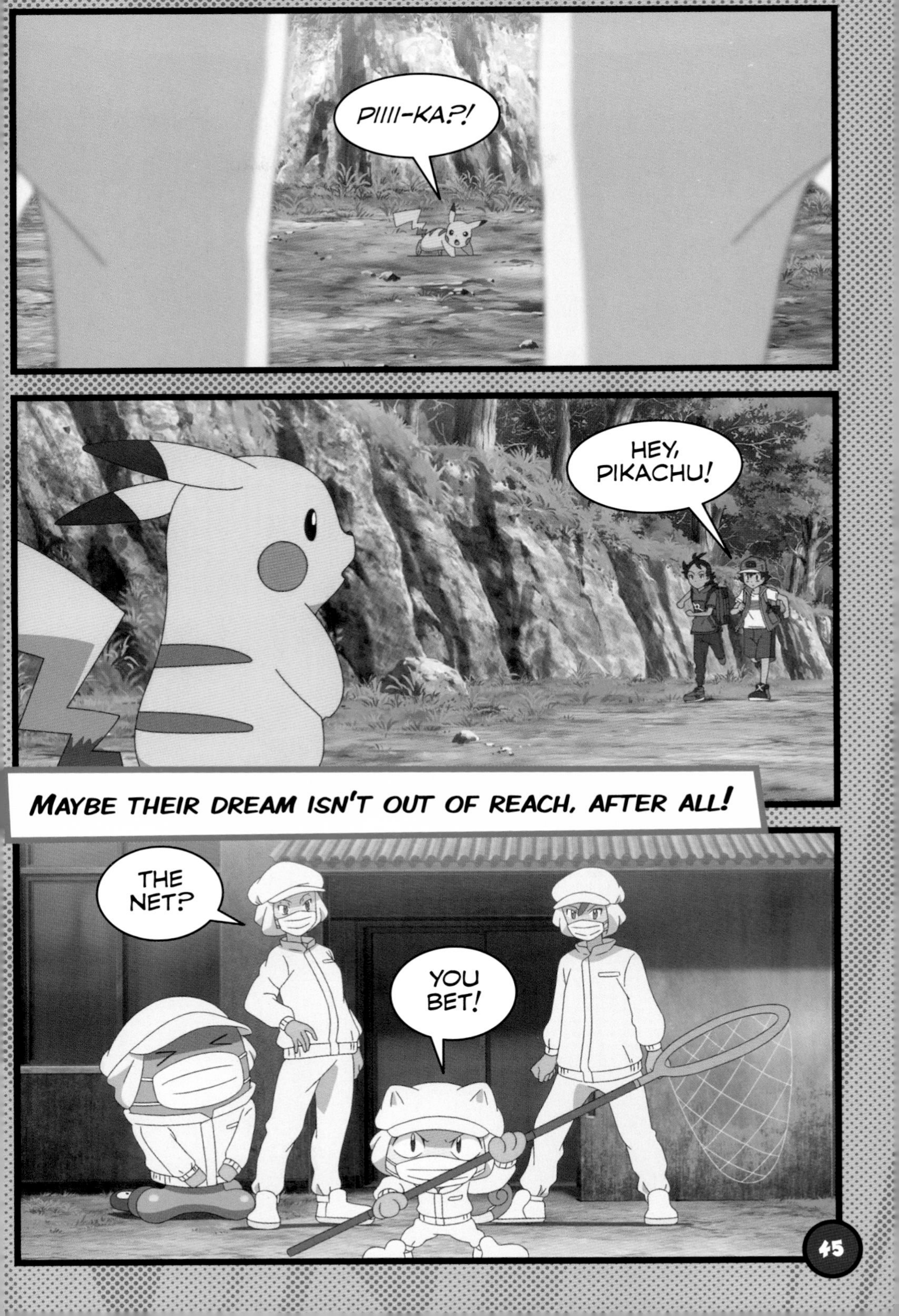
PIIII-KA?!
HEY, PIKACHU!
MAYBE THEIR DREAM ISN'T OUT OF REACH, AFTER ALL!
THE NET?
YOU BET!

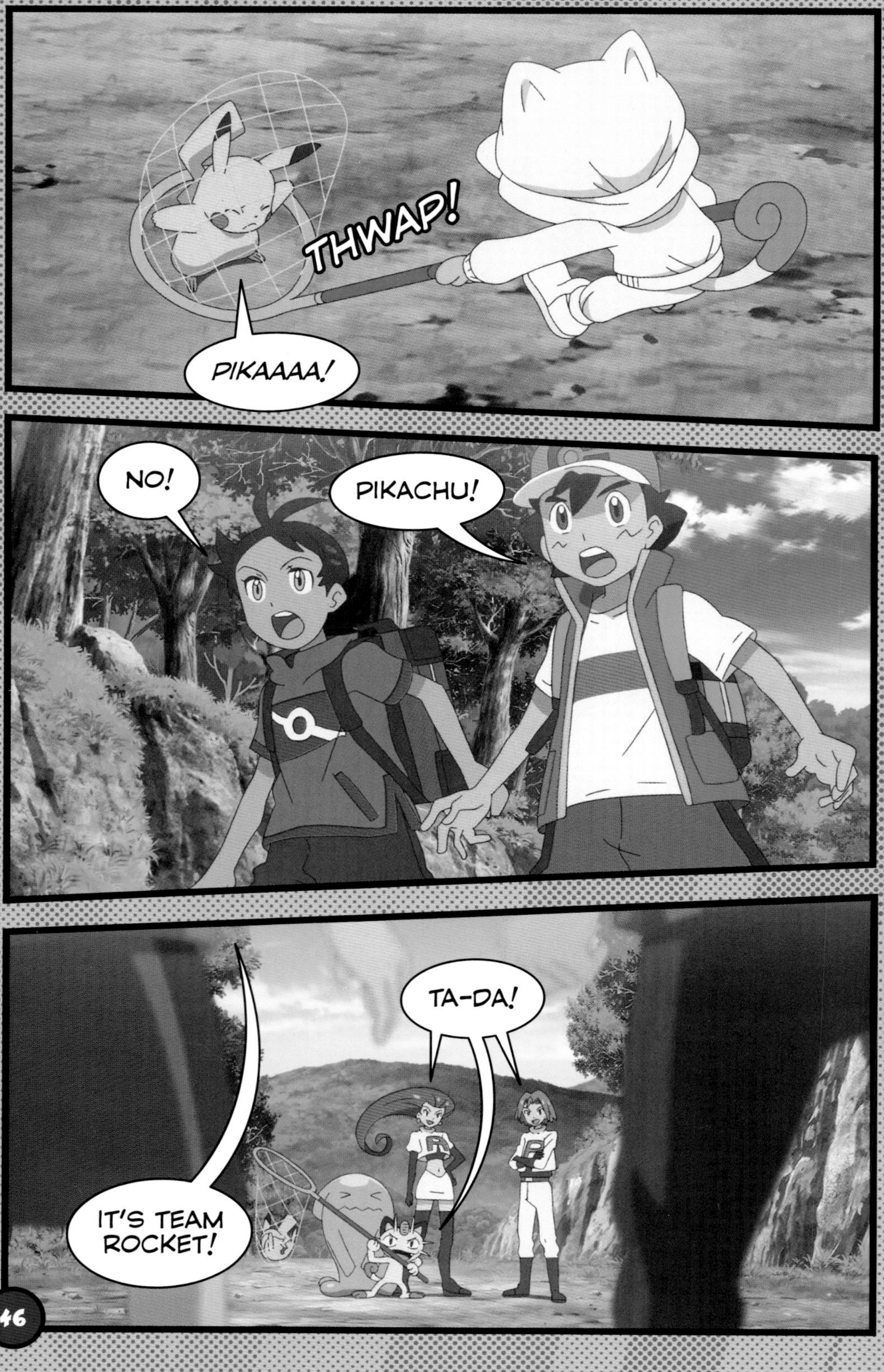
THWAP!
PIKAAAA!
NO!
PIKACHU!
TA-DA!
IT'S TEAM ROCKET!

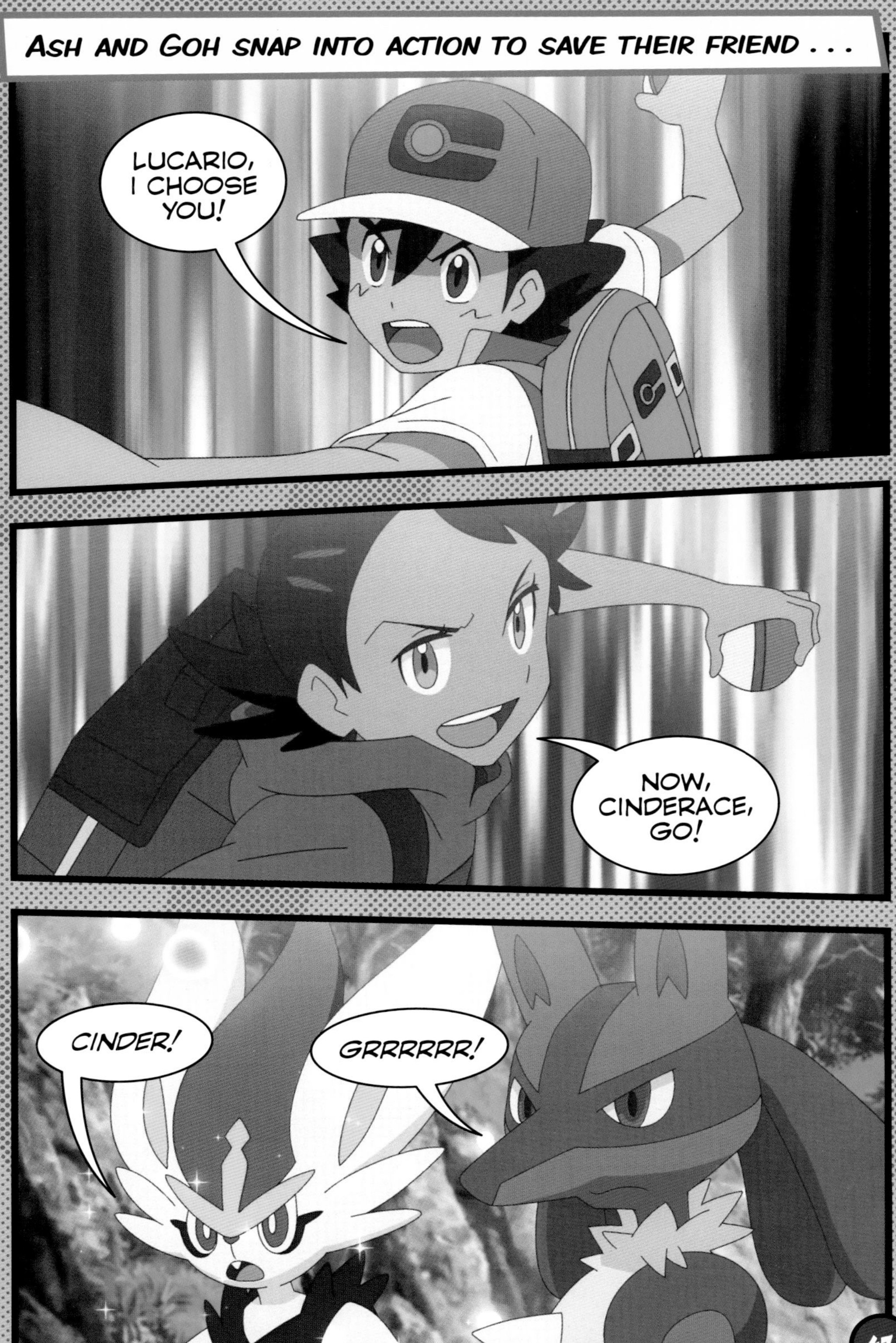
ASH AND GOH SNAP INTO ACTION TO SAVE THEIR FRIEND . . .
LUCARIO, I CHOOSE YOU!
NOW, CINDERACE, GO!
CINDER!
GRRRRRR!

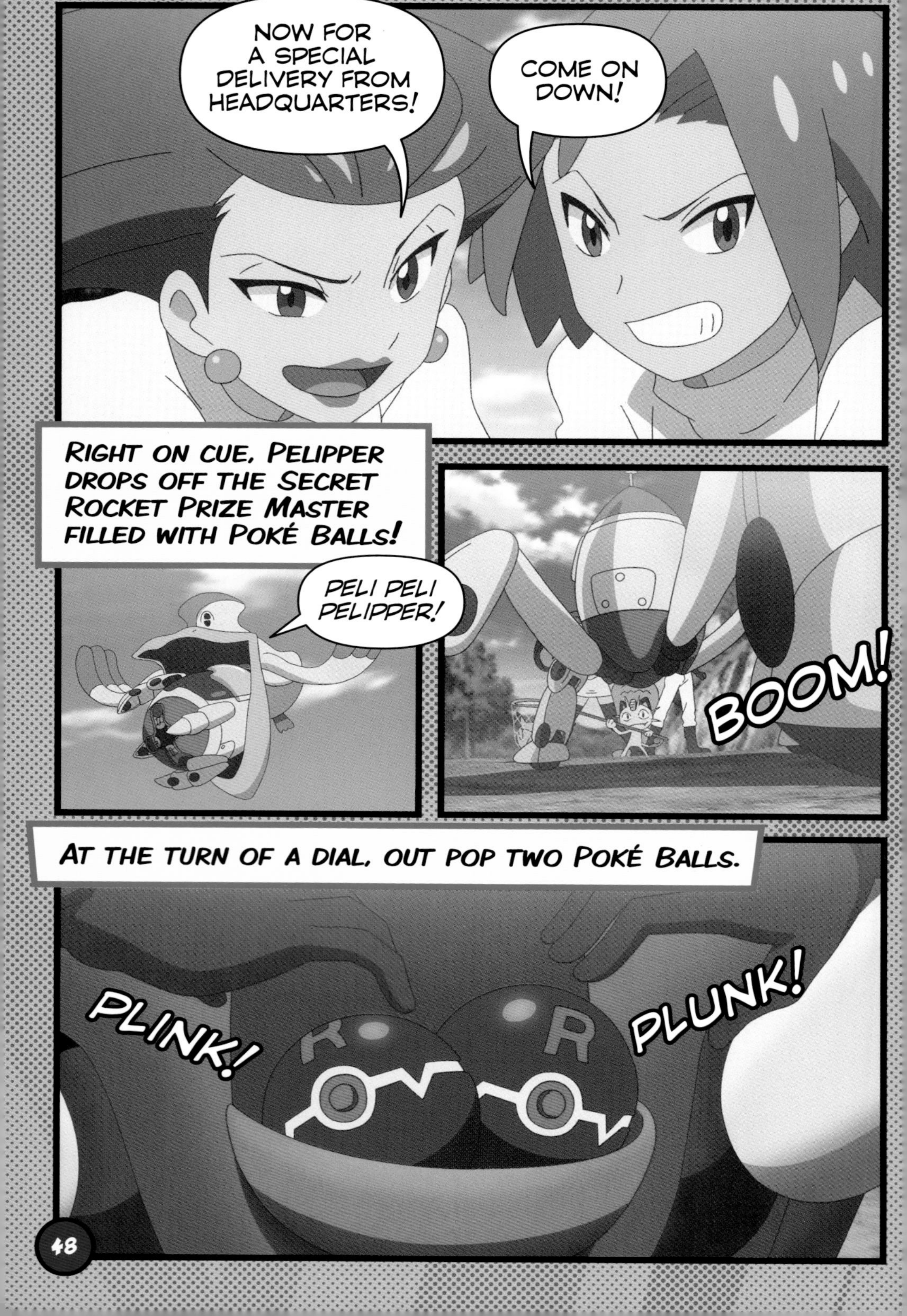
NOW FOR A SPECIAL DELIVERY FROM HEADQUARTERS!
COME ON DOWN!
RIGHT ON CUE, PELIPPER DROPS OFF THE SECRET ROCKET PRIZE MASTER FILLED WITH POKÉ BALLS!
PELI PELI PELIPPER!
BOOM!
AT THE TURN OF A DIAL, OUT POP TWO POKÉ BALLS.
PLINK!
PLUNK!

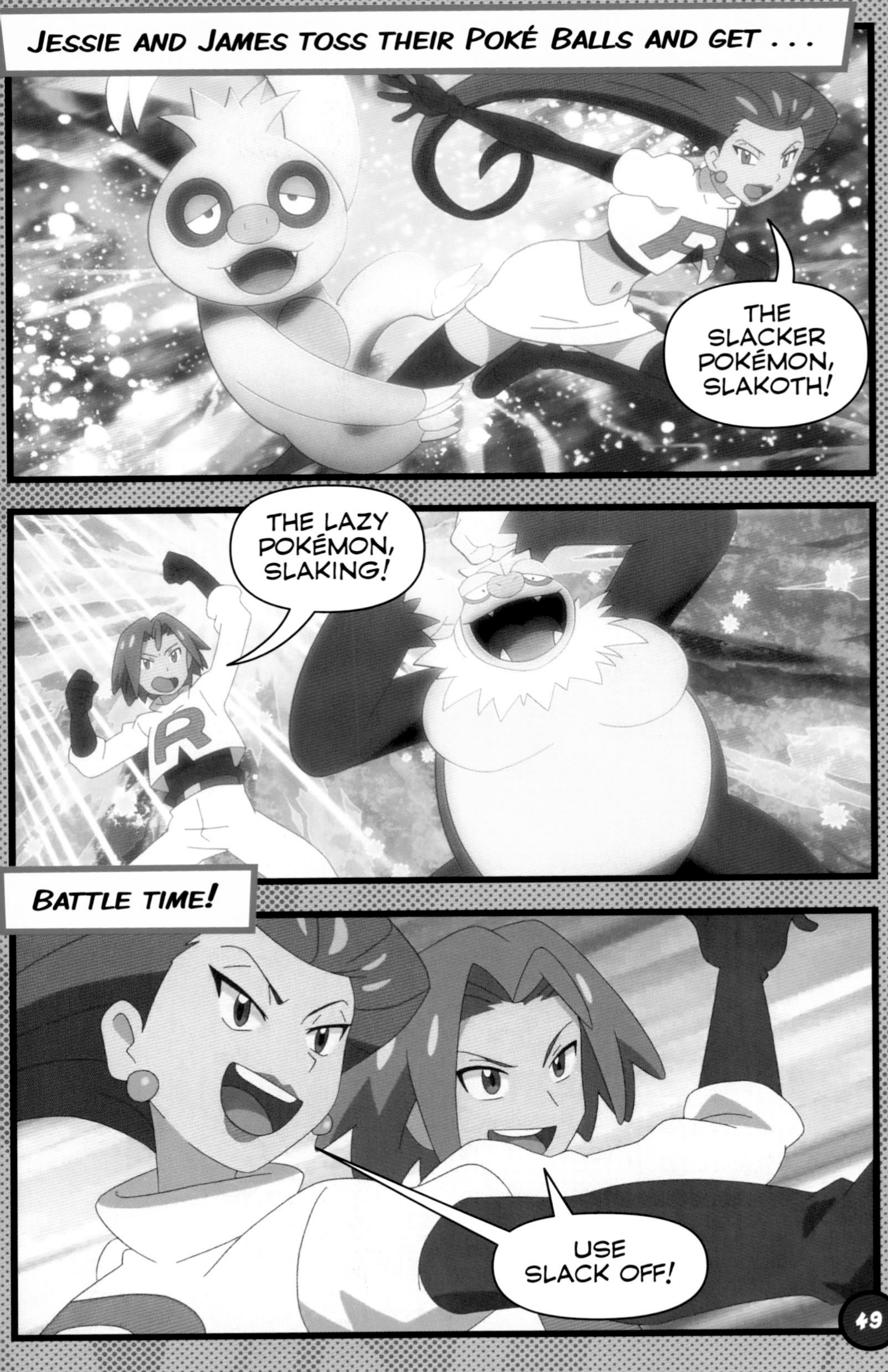
Jessie and James toss their Poké Balls and get . . .
THE SLACKER POKÉMON, SLAKOTH!
THE LAZY POKÉMON, SLAKING!
Battle time!
USE SLACK OFF!

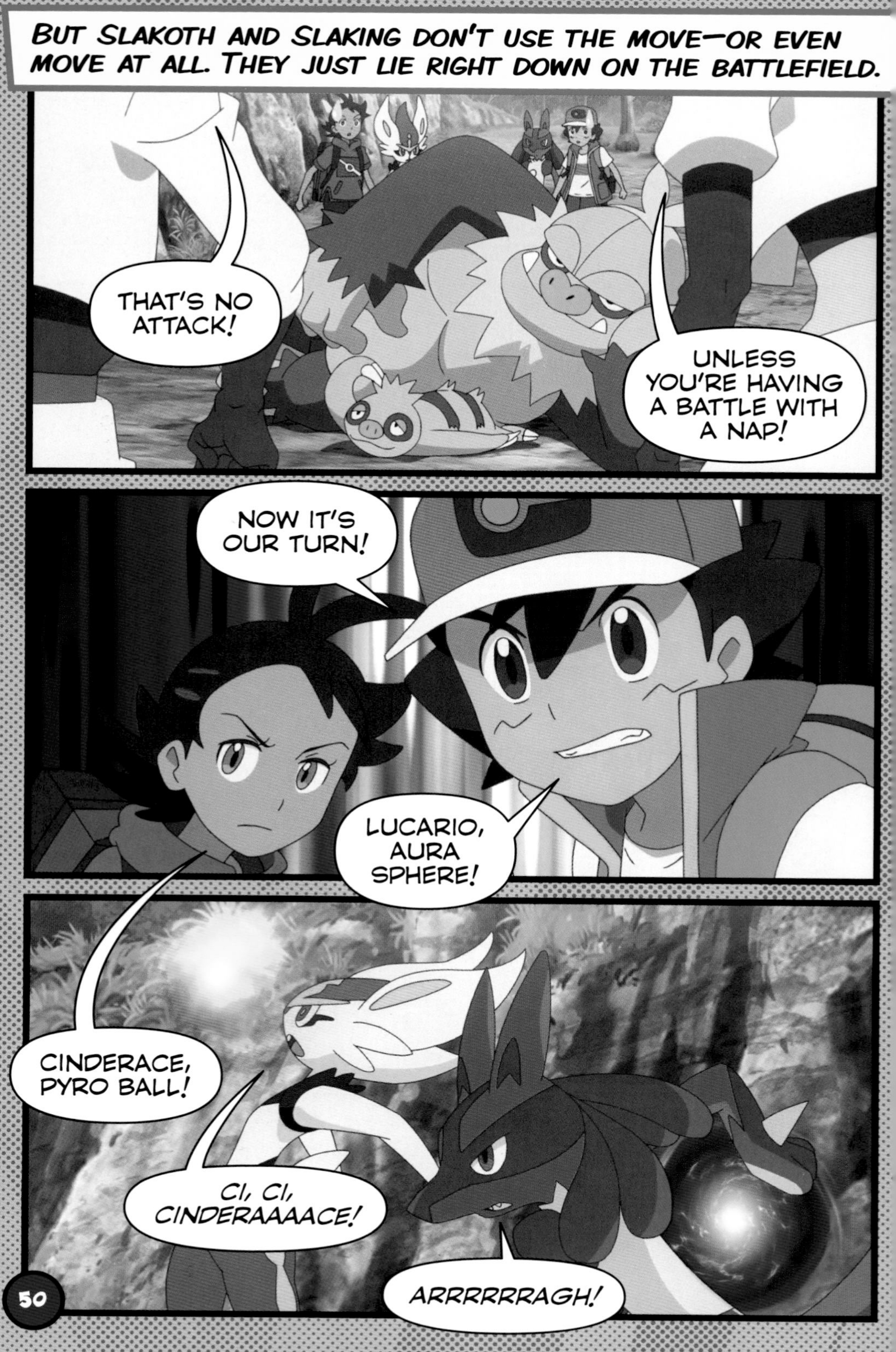
BUT SLAKOTH AND SLAKING DON'T USE THE MOVE—OR EVEN MOVE AT ALL. THEY JUST LIE RIGHT DOWN ON THE BATTLEFIELD.
THAT'S NO ATTACK!
UNLESS YOU'RE HAVING A BATTLE WITH A NAP!
NOW IT'S OUR TURN!
LUCARIO, AURA SPHERE!
CINDERACE, PYRO BALL!
CI, CI, CINDERAAAACE!
ARRRRRRAGH!

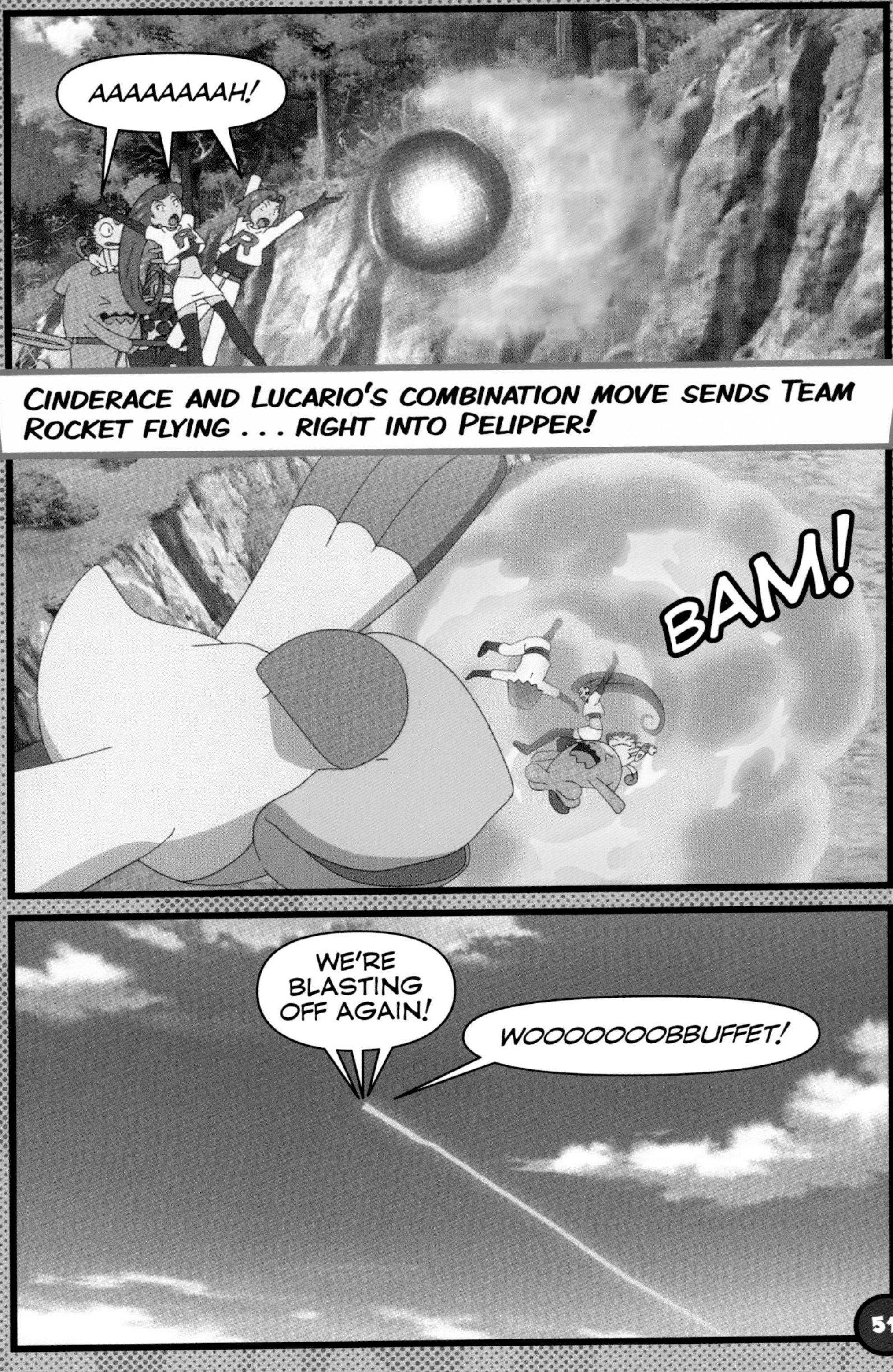
AAAAAAAAH!
CINDERACE AND LUCARIO'S COMBINATION MOVE SENDS TEAM ROCKET FLYING . . . RIGHT INTO PELIPPER!
BAM!
WE'RE BLASTING OFF AGAIN!
WOOOOOOOBBUFFET!

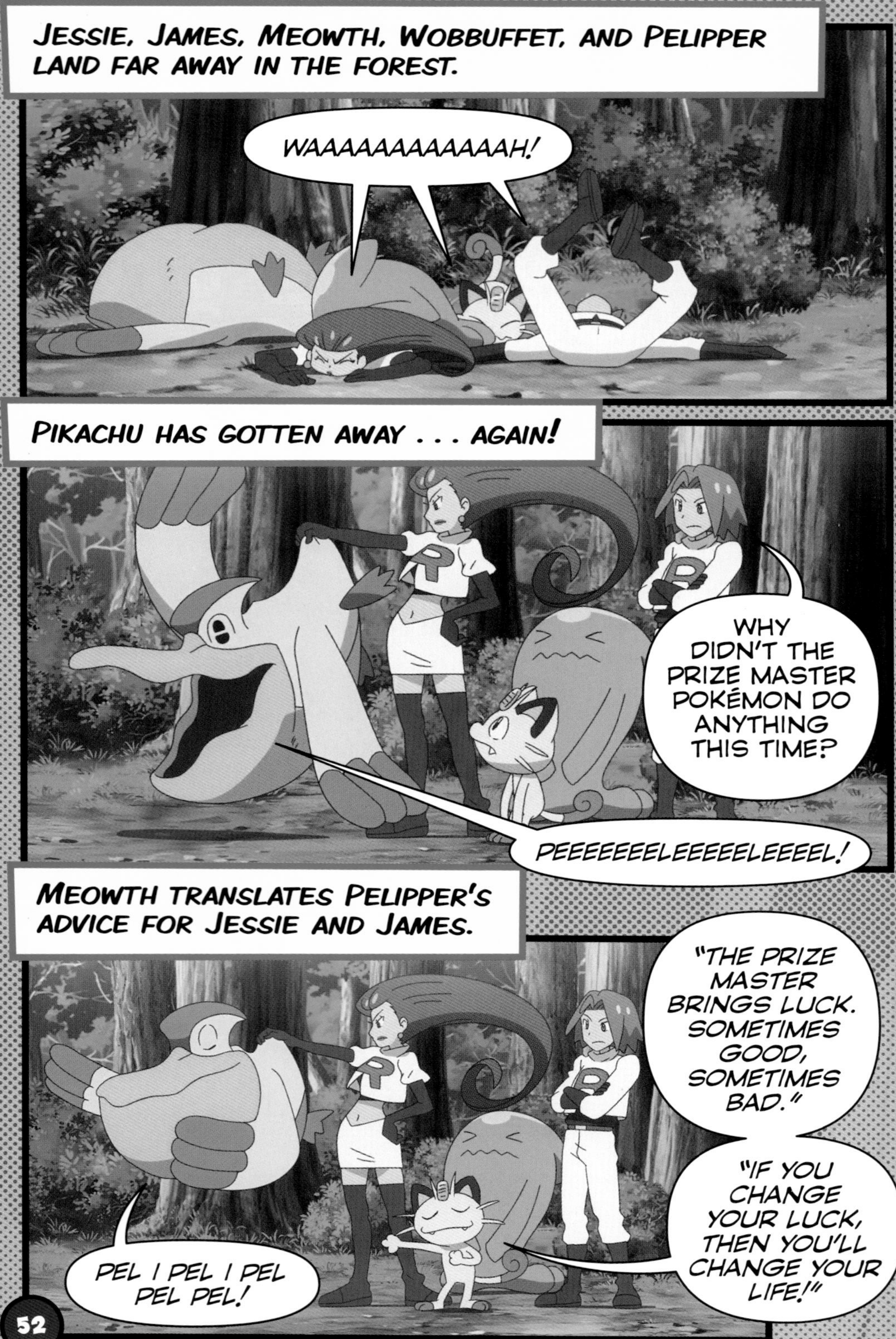
JESSIE, JAMES, MEOWTH, WOBBUFFET, AND PELIPPER LAND FAR AWAY IN THE FOREST.
WAAAAAAAAAAAAAH!
PIKACHU HAS GOTTEN AWAY . . . AGAIN!
WHY DIDN'T THE PRIZE MASTER POKÉMON DO ANYTHING THIS TIME?
PEEEEEEELEEEEELEEEEL!
MEOWTH TRANSLATES PELIPPER'S ADVICE FOR JESSIE AND JAMES.
PEL I PEL I PEL PEL PEL!
"THE PRIZE MASTER BRINGS LUCK. SOMETIMES GOOD, SOMETIMES BAD."
"IF YOU CHANGE YOUR LUCK, THEN YOU'LL CHANGE YOUR LIFE!"

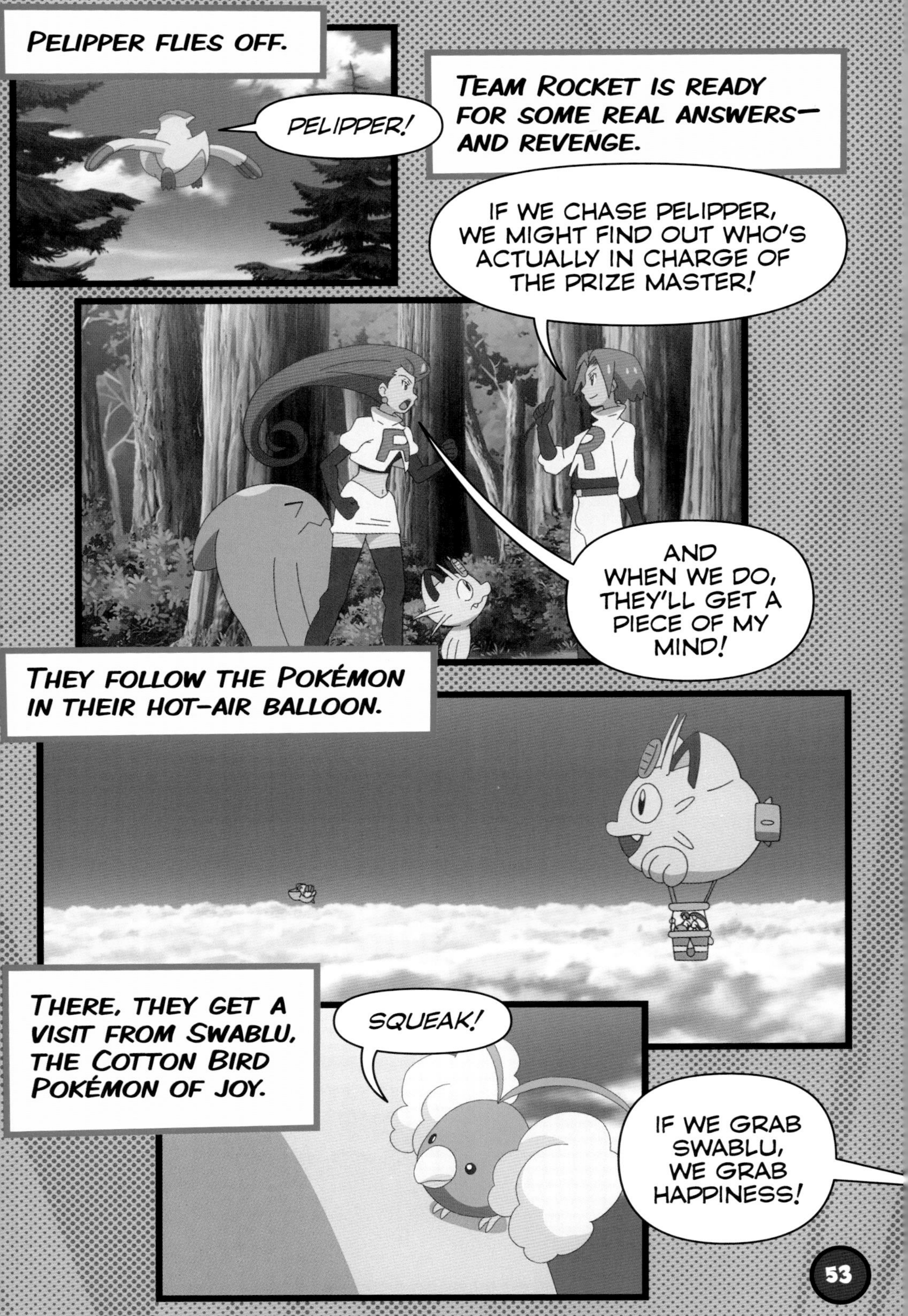

PELIPPER FLIES OFF.
PELIPPER!
TEAM ROCKET IS READY FOR SOME REAL ANSWERS—AND REVENGE.
IF WE CHASE PELIPPER, WE MIGHT FIND OUT WHO'S ACTUALLY IN CHARGE OF THE PRIZE MASTER!
AND WHEN WE DO, THEY'LL GET A PIECE OF MY MIND!
THEY FOLLOW THE POKÉMON IN THEIR HOT-AIR BALLOON.
THERE, THEY GET A VISIT FROM SWABLU, THE COTTON BIRD POKÉMON OF JOY.
SQUEAK!
IF WE GRAB SWABLU, WE GRAB HAPPINESS!

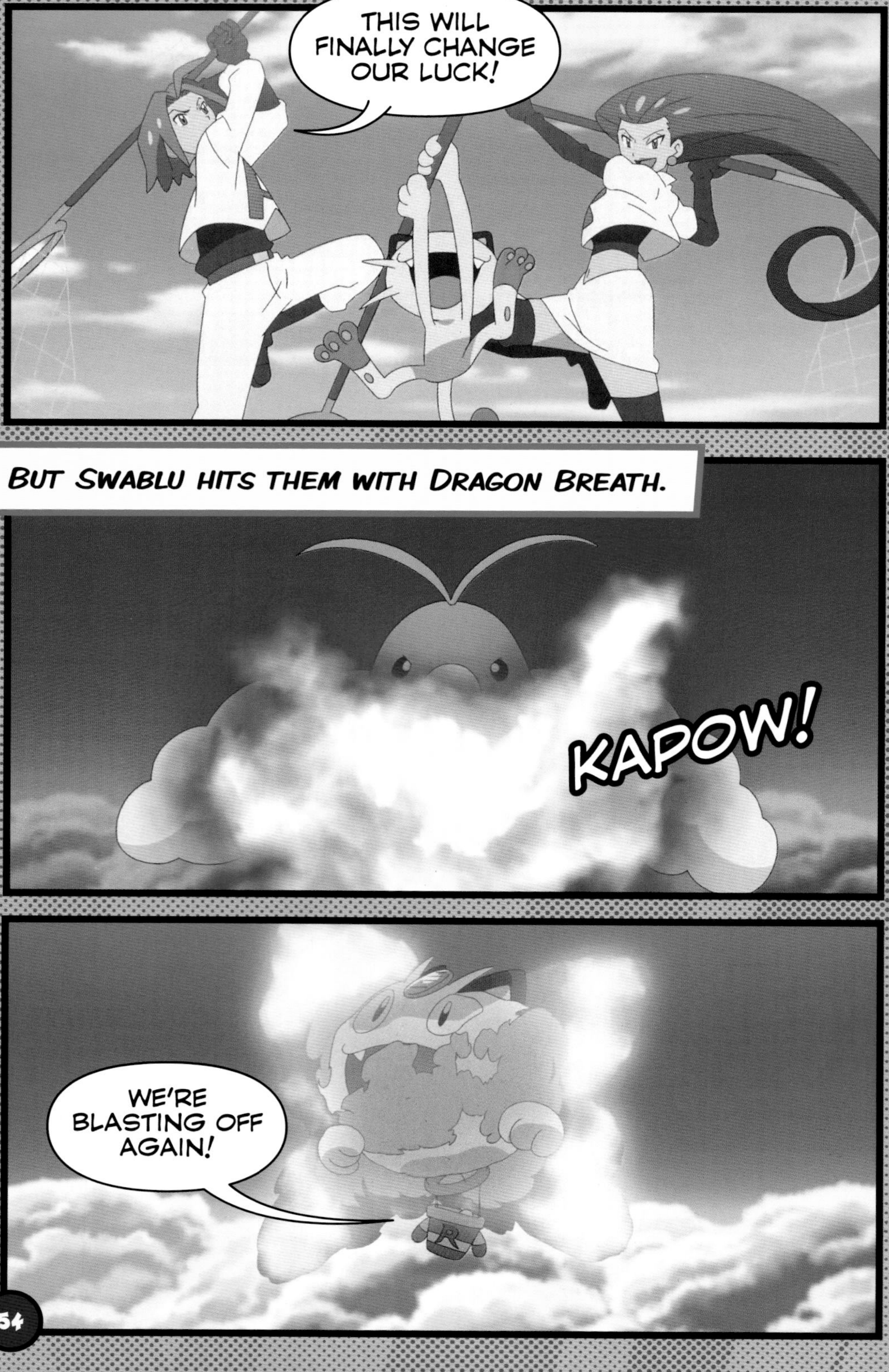
THIS WILL FINALLY CHANGE OUR LUCK!
BUT SWABLU HITS THEM WITH DRAGON BREATH.
KAPOW!
WE'RE BLASTING OFF AGAIN!

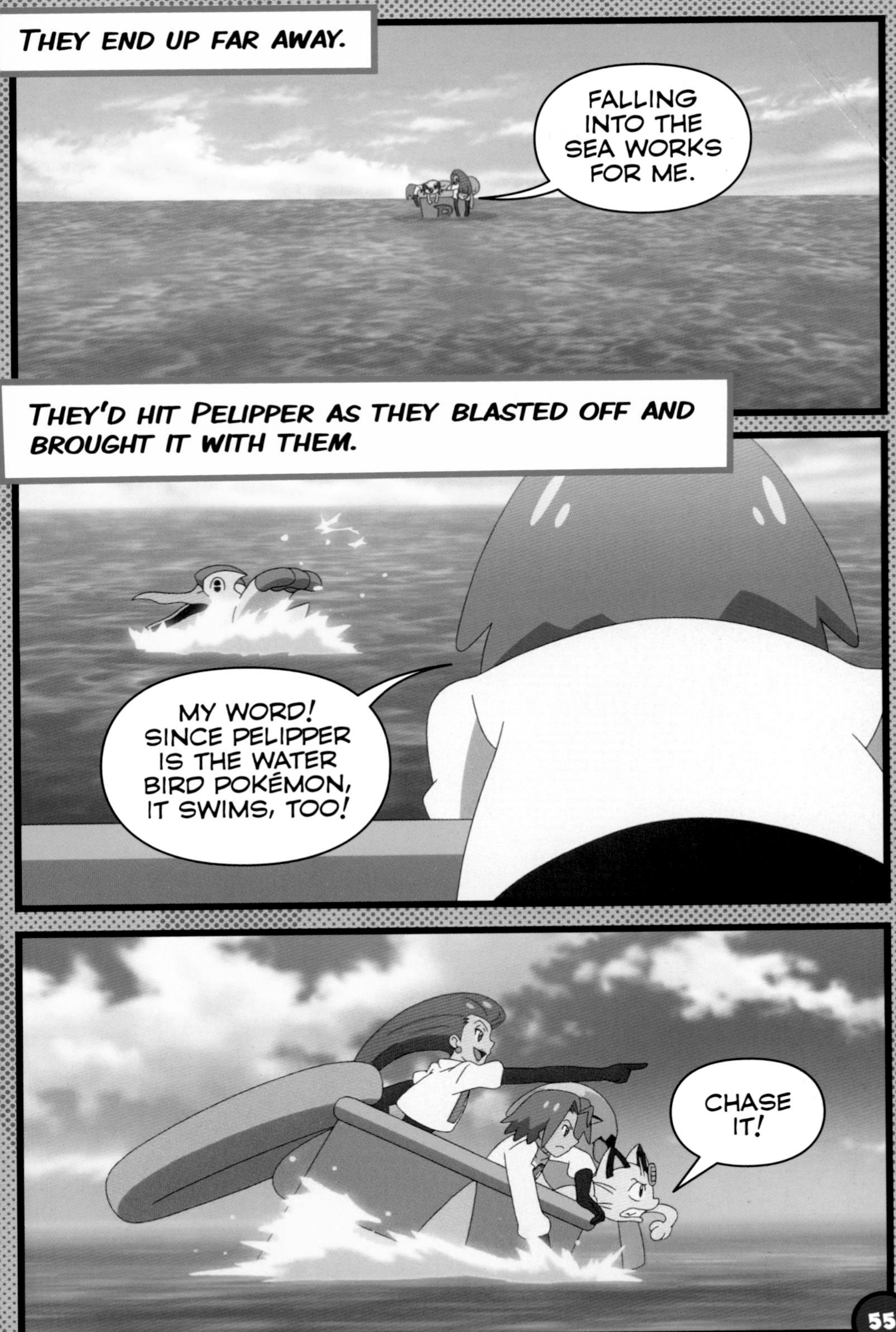
THEY END UP FAR AWAY.
FALLING INTO THE SEA WORKS FOR ME.
THEY'D HIT PELIPPER AS THEY BLASTED OFF AND BROUGHT IT WITH THEM.
MY WORD! SINCE PELIPPER IS THE WATER BIRD POKÉMON, IT SWIMS, TOO!
CHASE IT!

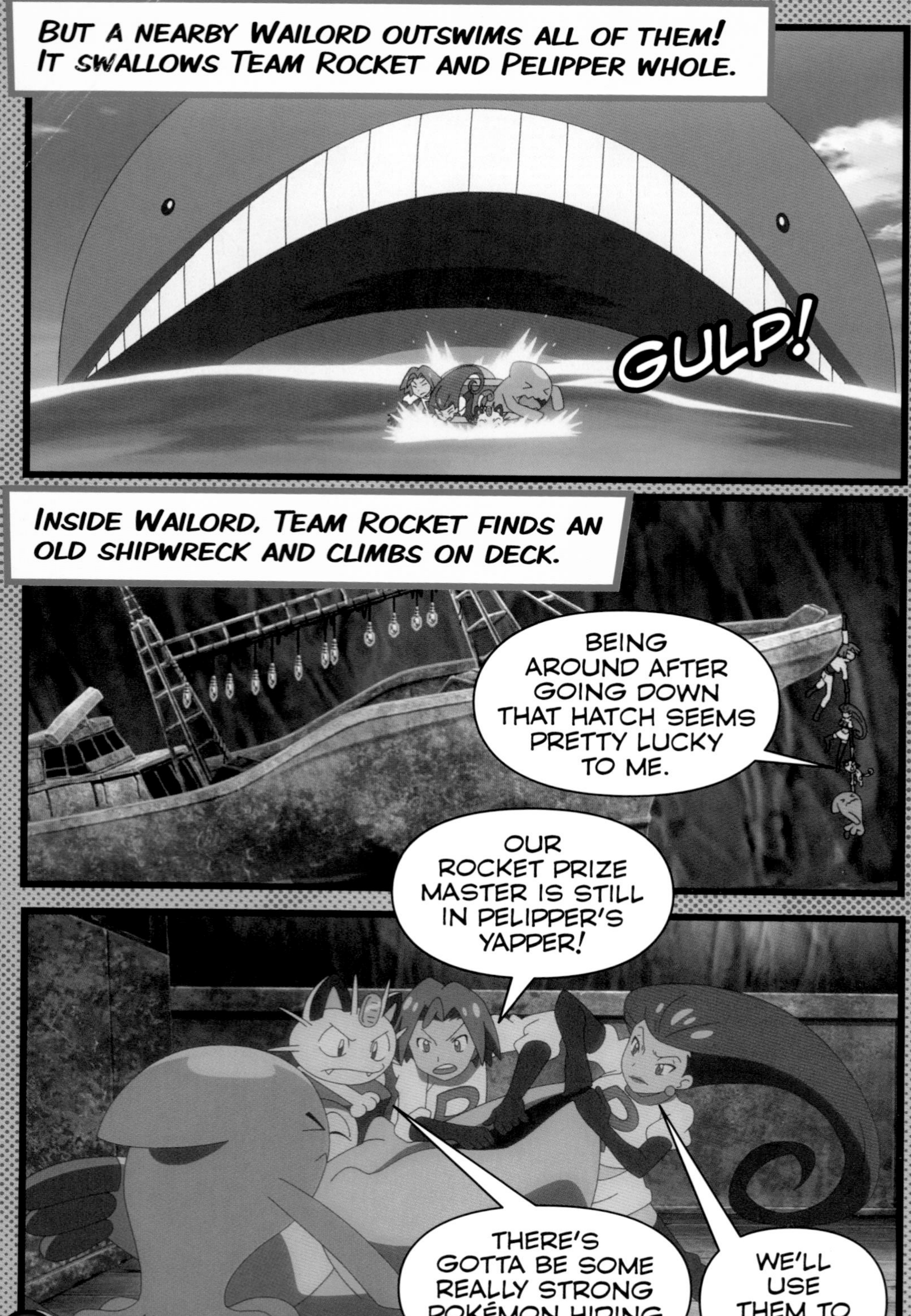
BUT A NEARBY WAILORD OUTSWIMS ALL OF THEM! IT SWALLOWS TEAM ROCKET AND PELIPPER WHOLE.
GULP!
INSIDE WAILORD, TEAM ROCKET FINDS AN OLD SHIPWRECK AND CLIMBS ON DECK.
BEING AROUND AFTER GOING DOWN THAT HATCH SEEMS PRETTY LUCKY TO ME.
OUR ROCKET PRIZE MASTER IS STILL IN PELIPPER'S YAPPER!
THERE'S GOTTA BE SOME REALLY STRONG POKÉMON HIDING IN THERE!
WE'LL USE THEM TO ESCAPE!

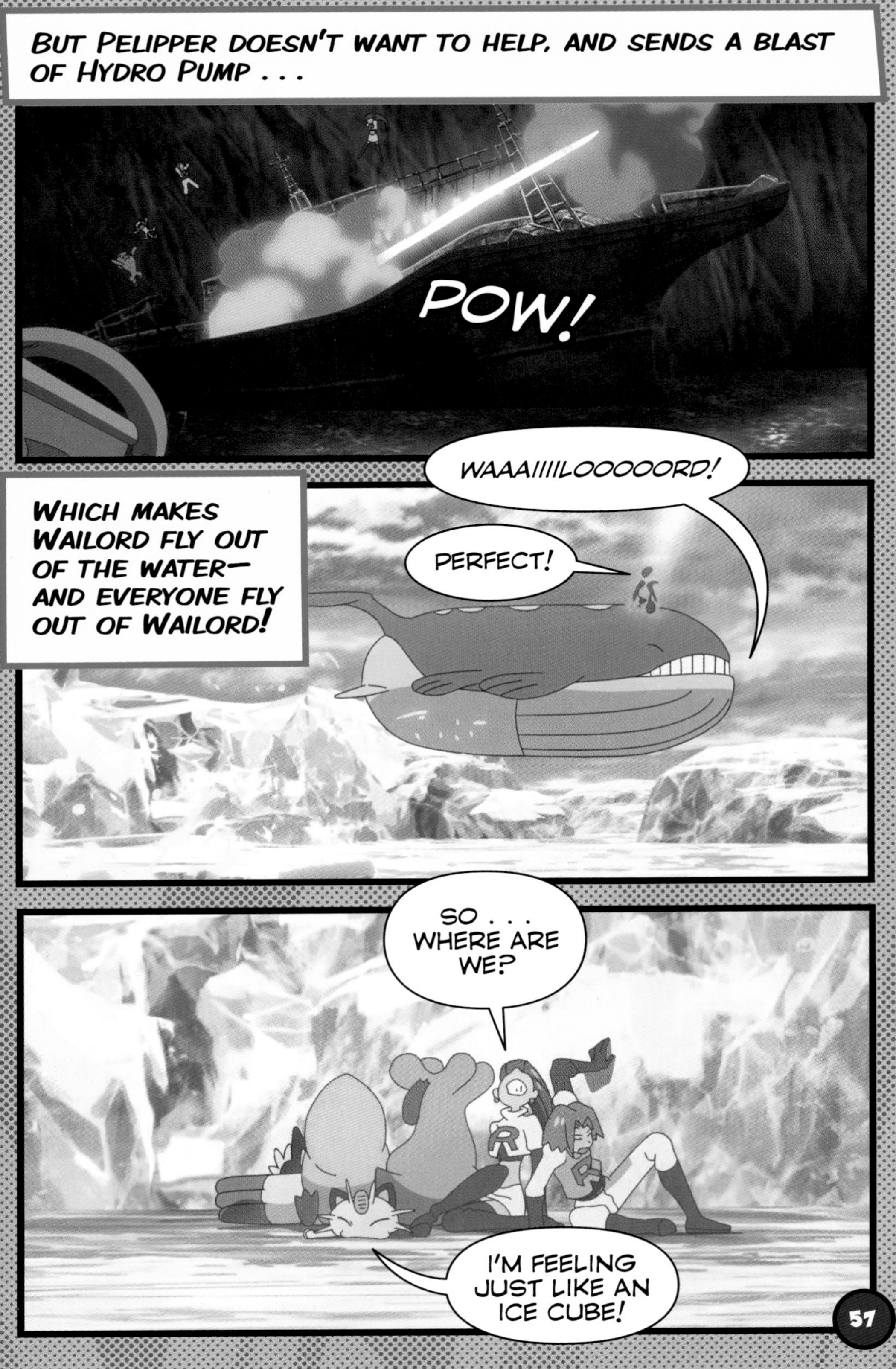
But Pelipper doesn't want to help, and sends a blast of Hydro Pump . . .
POW!
Which makes Wailord fly out of the water— and everyone fly out of Wailord!
WAAAIIIILOOOOORD!
PERFECT!
SO . . . WHERE ARE WE?
I'M FEELING JUST LIKE AN ICE CUBE!

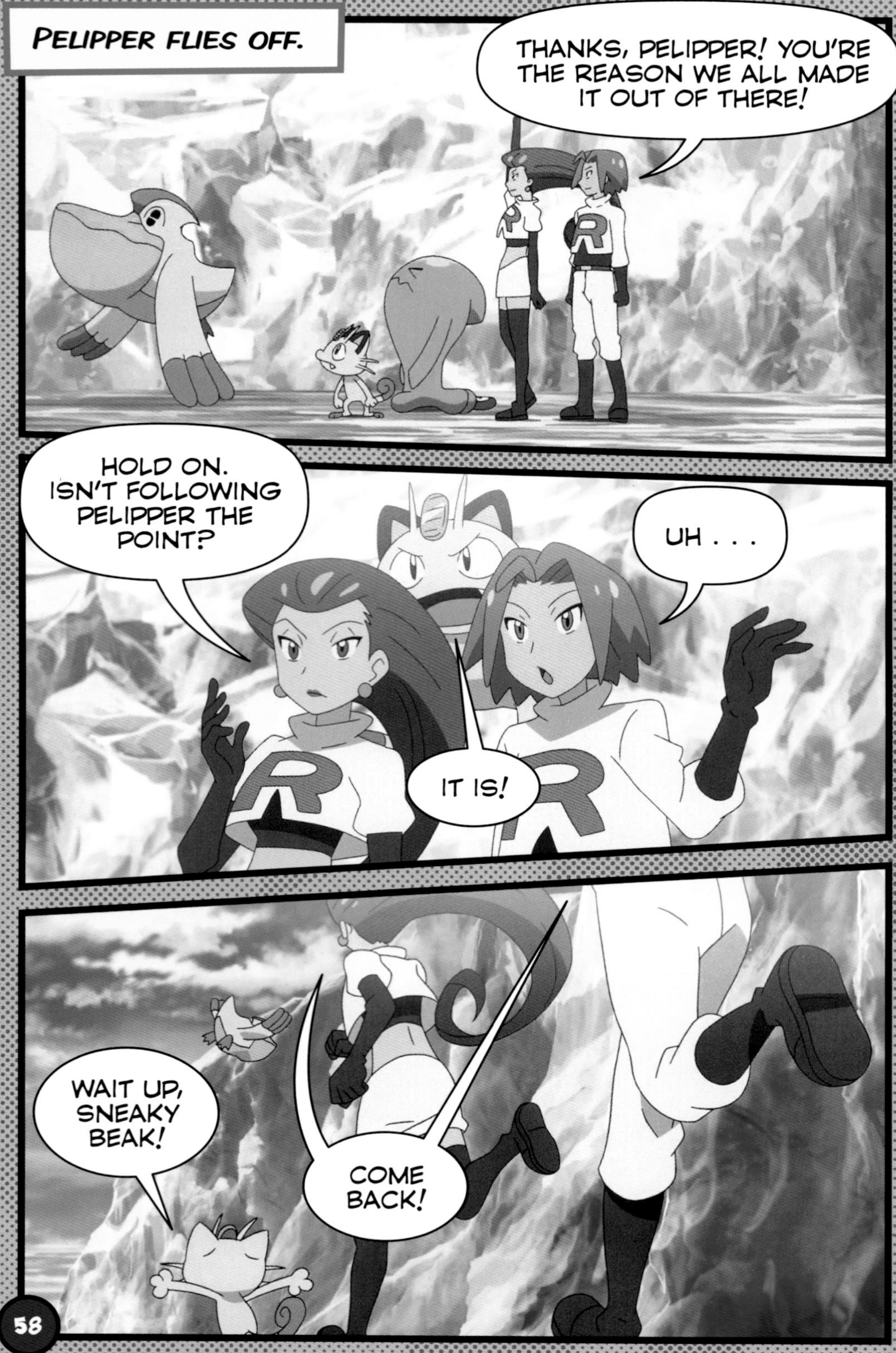
PELIPPER FLIES OFF.
THANKS, PELIPPER! YOU'RE THE REASON WE ALL MADE IT OUT OF THERE!
HOLD ON. ISN'T FOLLOWING PELIPPER THE POINT?
UH . . .
IT IS!
WAIT UP, SNEAKY BEAK!
COME BACK!

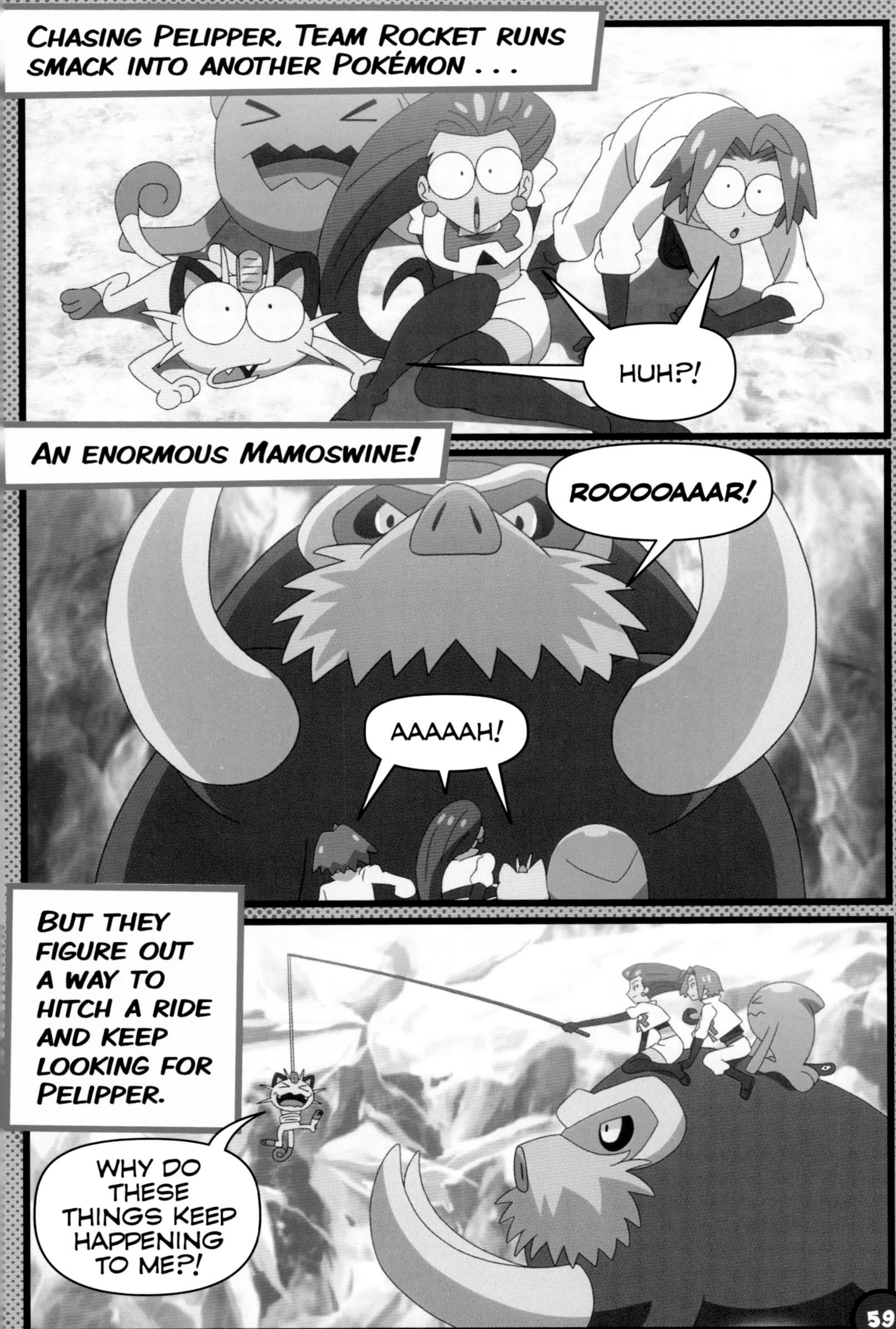
CHASING PELIPPER, TEAM ROCKET RUNS SMACK INTO ANOTHER POKÉMON . . .
HUH?!
AN ENORMOUS MAMOSWINE!
ROOOOAAAR!
AAAAAH!
BUT THEY FIGURE OUT A WAY TO HITCH A RIDE AND KEEP LOOKING FOR PELIPPER.
WHY DO THESE THINGS KEEP HAPPENING TO ME?!

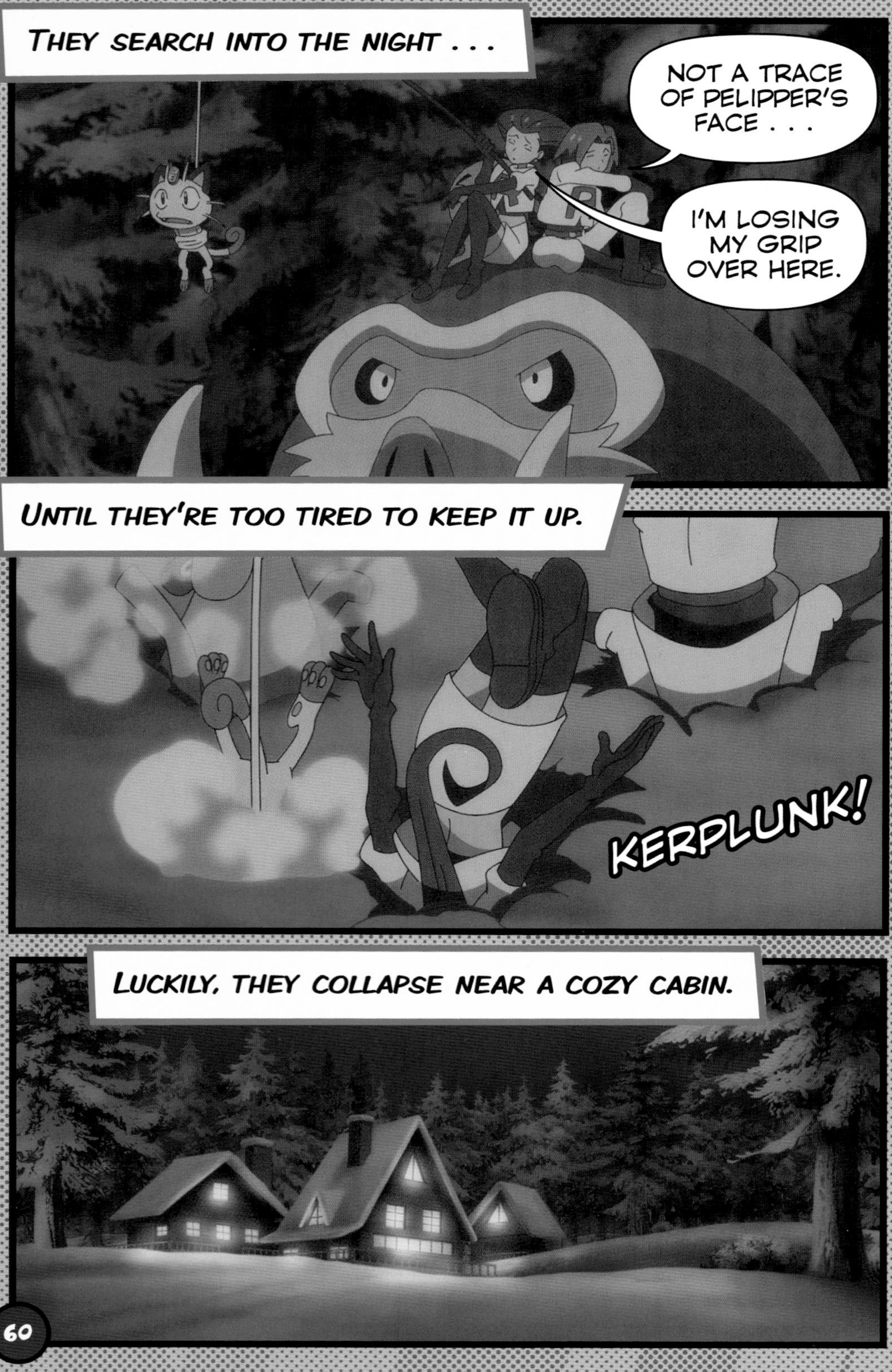
THEY SEARCH INTO THE NIGHT . . .
NOT A TRACE OF PELIPPER'S FACE . . .
I'M LOSING MY GRIP OVER HERE.
UNTIL THEY'RE TOO TIRED TO KEEP IT UP.
KERPLUNK!
LUCKILY, THEY COLLAPSE NEAR A COZY CABIN.

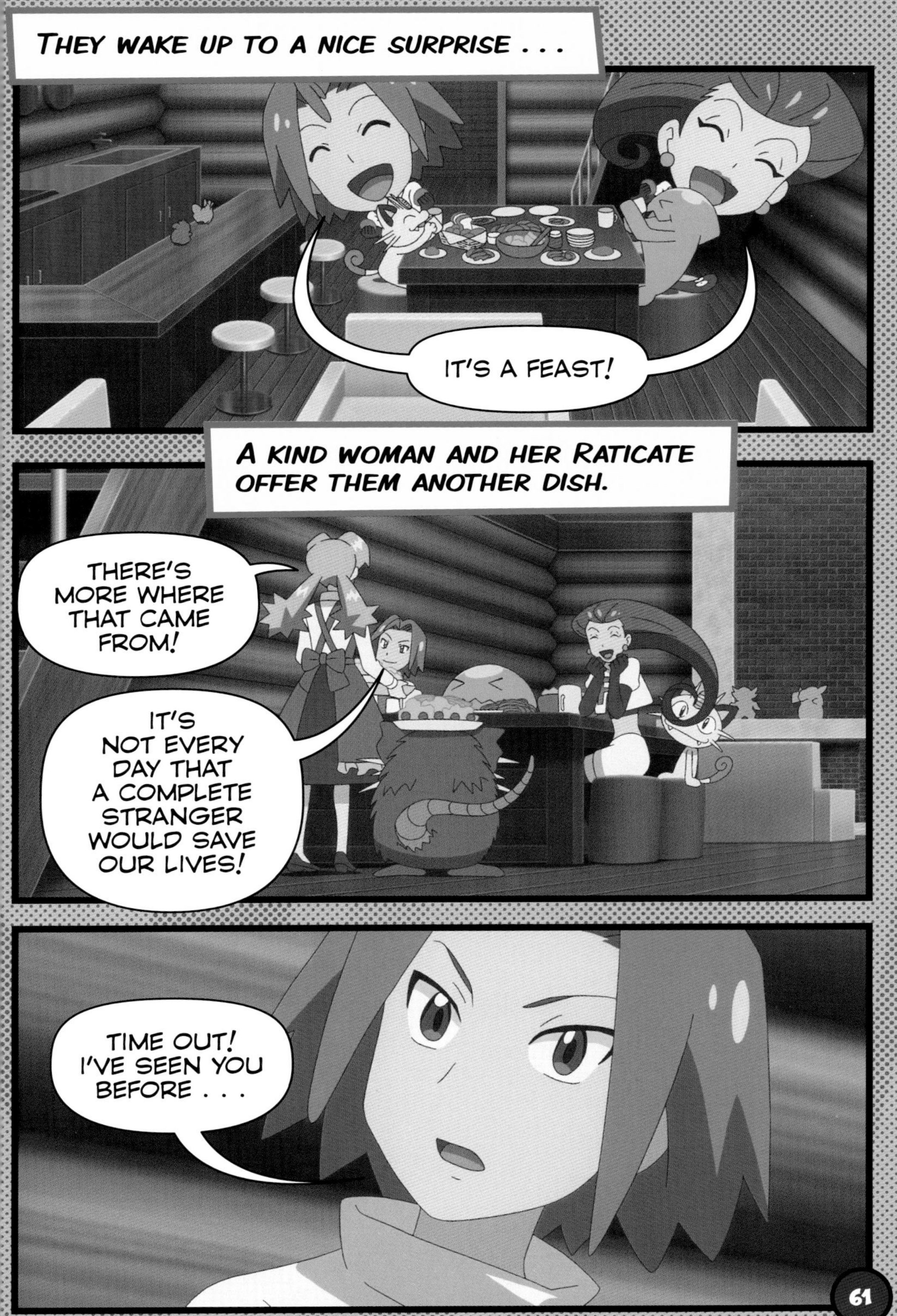
THEY WAKE UP TO A NICE SURPRISE . . .
IT'S A FEAST!
A KIND WOMAN AND HER RATICATE OFFER THEM ANOTHER DISH.
THERE'S MORE WHERE THAT CAME FROM!
IT'S NOT EVERY DAY THAT A COMPLETE STRANGER WOULD SAVE OUR LIVES!
TIME OUT! I'VE SEEN YOU BEFORE . . .

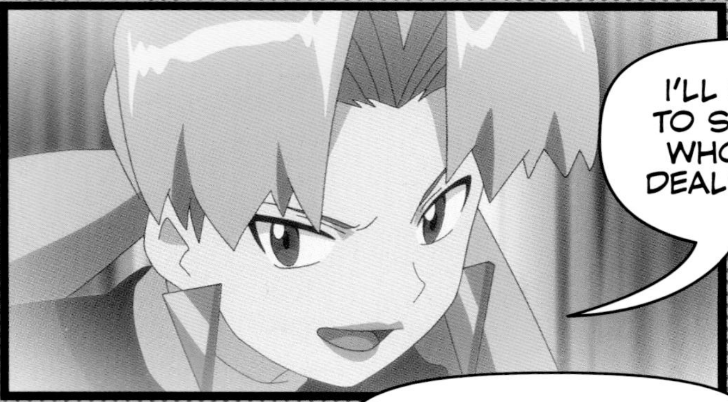
I'LL BE GLAD TO SHOW YOU WHO YOU'RE DEALING WITH.

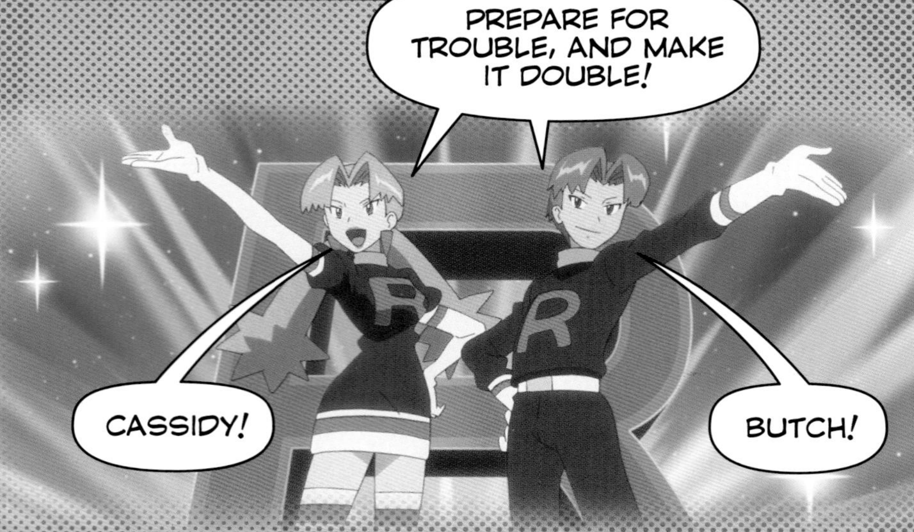
PREPARE FOR TROUBLE, AND MAKE IT DOUBLE!
CASSIDY!
BUTCH!

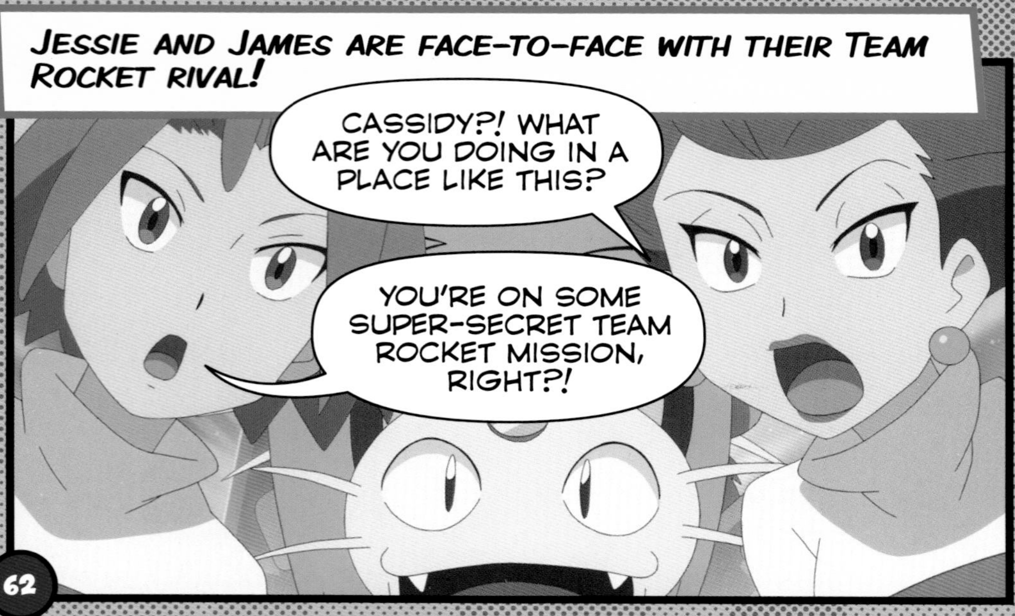
JESSIE AND JAMES ARE FACE-TO-FACE WITH THEIR TEAM ROCKET RIVAL!
CASSIDY?! WHAT ARE YOU DOING IN A PLACE LIKE THIS?
YOU'RE ON SOME SUPER-SECRET TEAM ROCKET MISSION, RIGHT?!

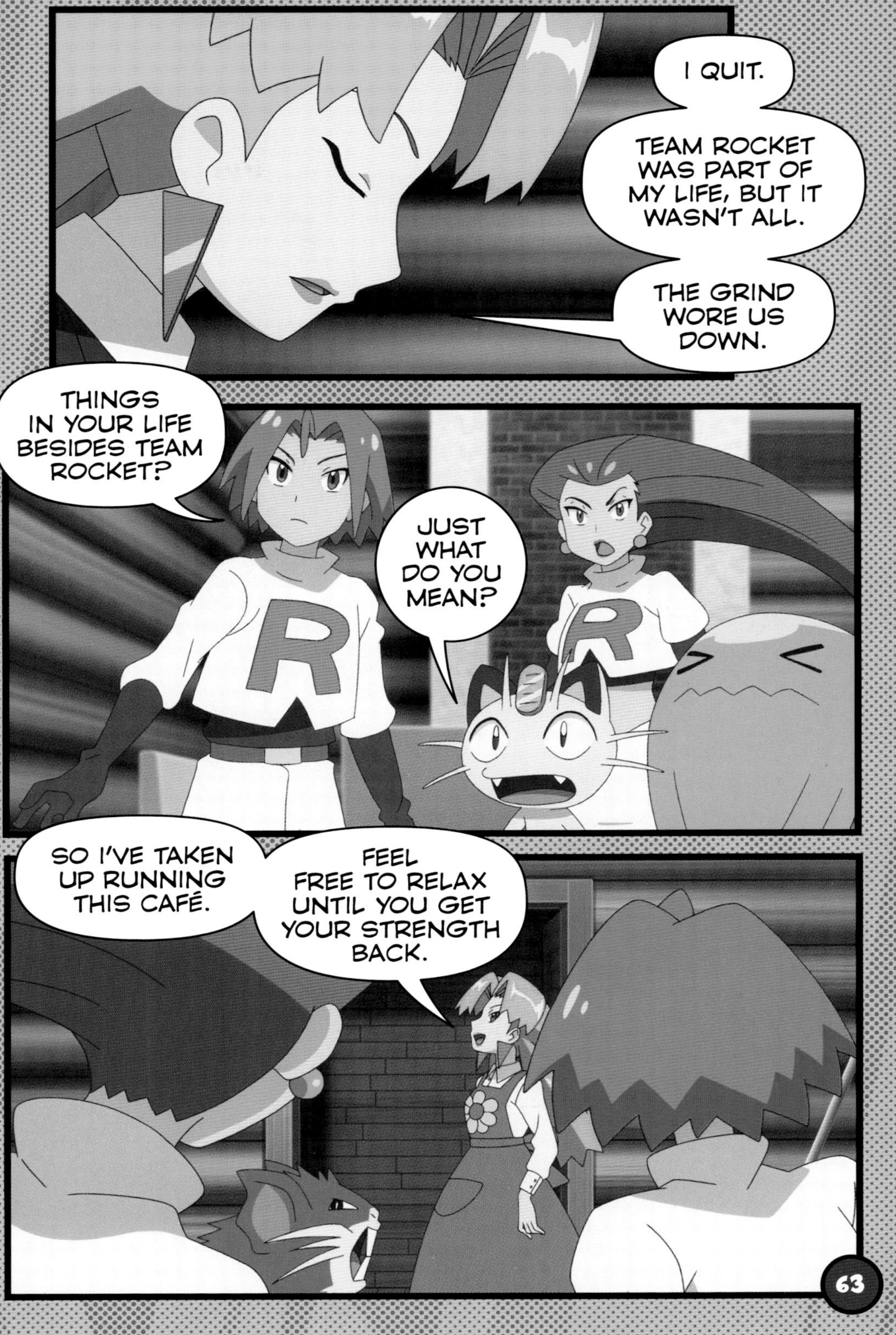

I QUIT.
TEAM ROCKET WAS PART OF MY LIFE, BUT IT WASN'T ALL.
THE GRIND WORE US DOWN.
THINGS IN YOUR LIFE BESIDES TEAM ROCKET?
JUST WHAT DO YOU MEAN?
SO I'VE TAKEN UP RUNNING THIS CAFÉ.
FEEL FREE TO RELAX UNTIL YOU GET YOUR STRENGTH BACK.

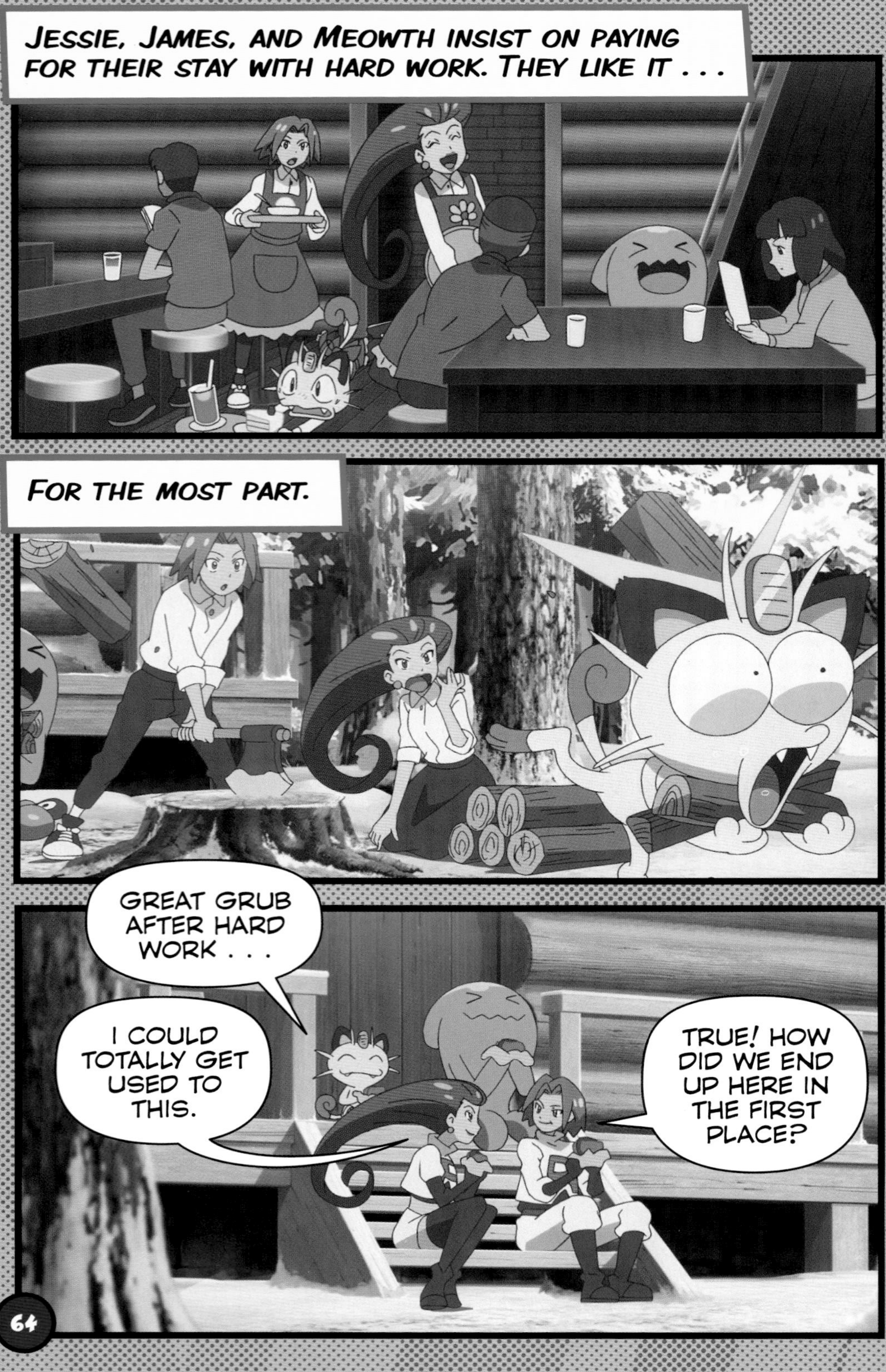
JESSIE, JAMES, AND MEOWTH INSIST ON PAYING FOR THEIR STAY WITH HARD WORK. THEY LIKE IT . . .
FOR THE MOST PART.
GREAT GRUB AFTER HARD WORK . . .
I COULD TOTALLY GET USED TO THIS.
TRUE! HOW DID WE END UP HERE IN THE FIRST PLACE?

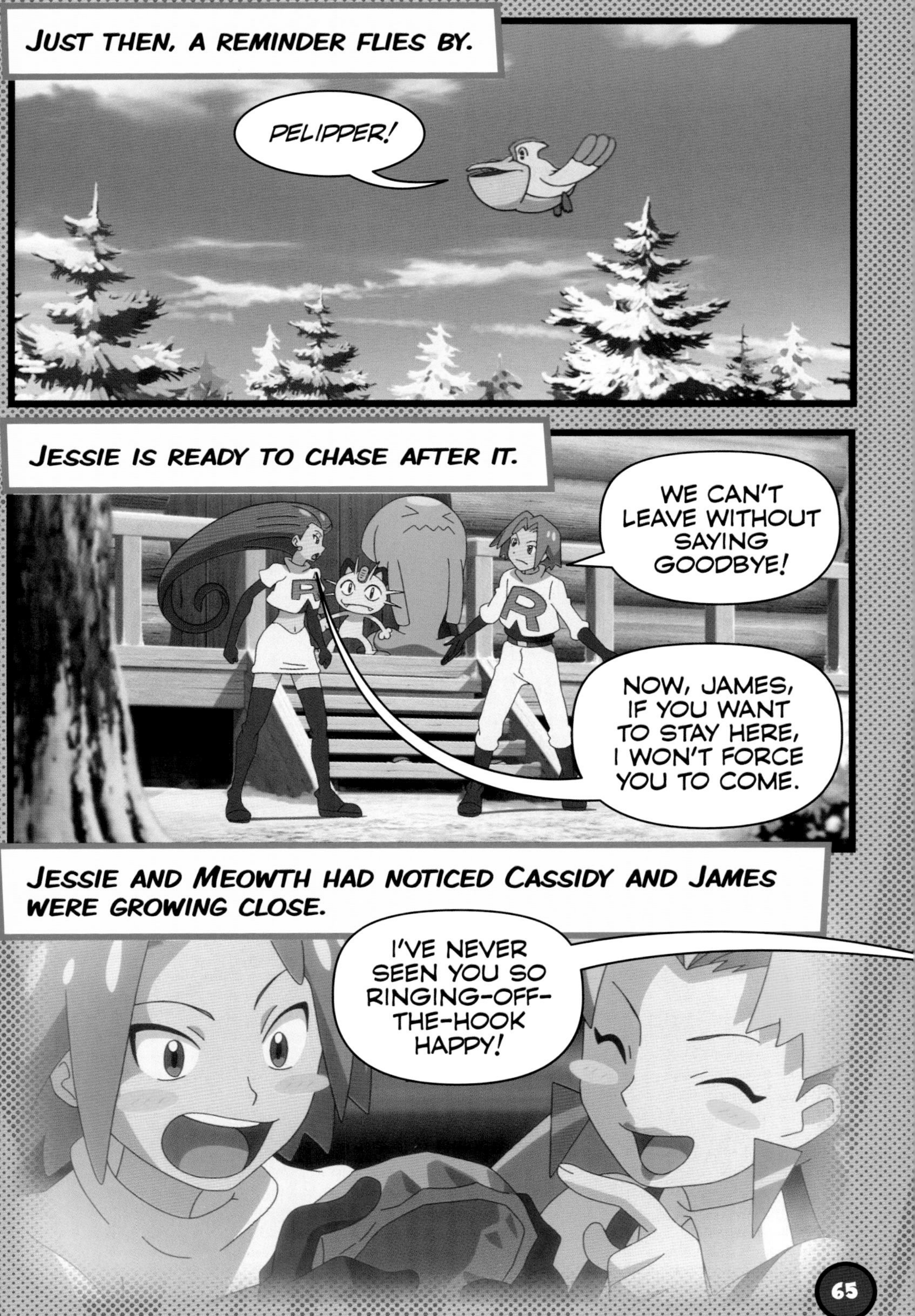
JUST THEN, A REMINDER FLIES BY.
PELIPPER!
JESSIE IS READY TO CHASE AFTER IT.
WE CAN'T LEAVE WITHOUT SAYING GOODBYE!
NOW, JAMES, IF YOU WANT TO STAY HERE, I WON'T FORCE YOU TO COME.
JESSIE AND MEOWTH HAD NOTICED CASSIDY AND JAMES WERE GROWING CLOSE.
I'VE NEVER SEEN YOU SO RINGING-OFF-THE-HOOK HAPPY!

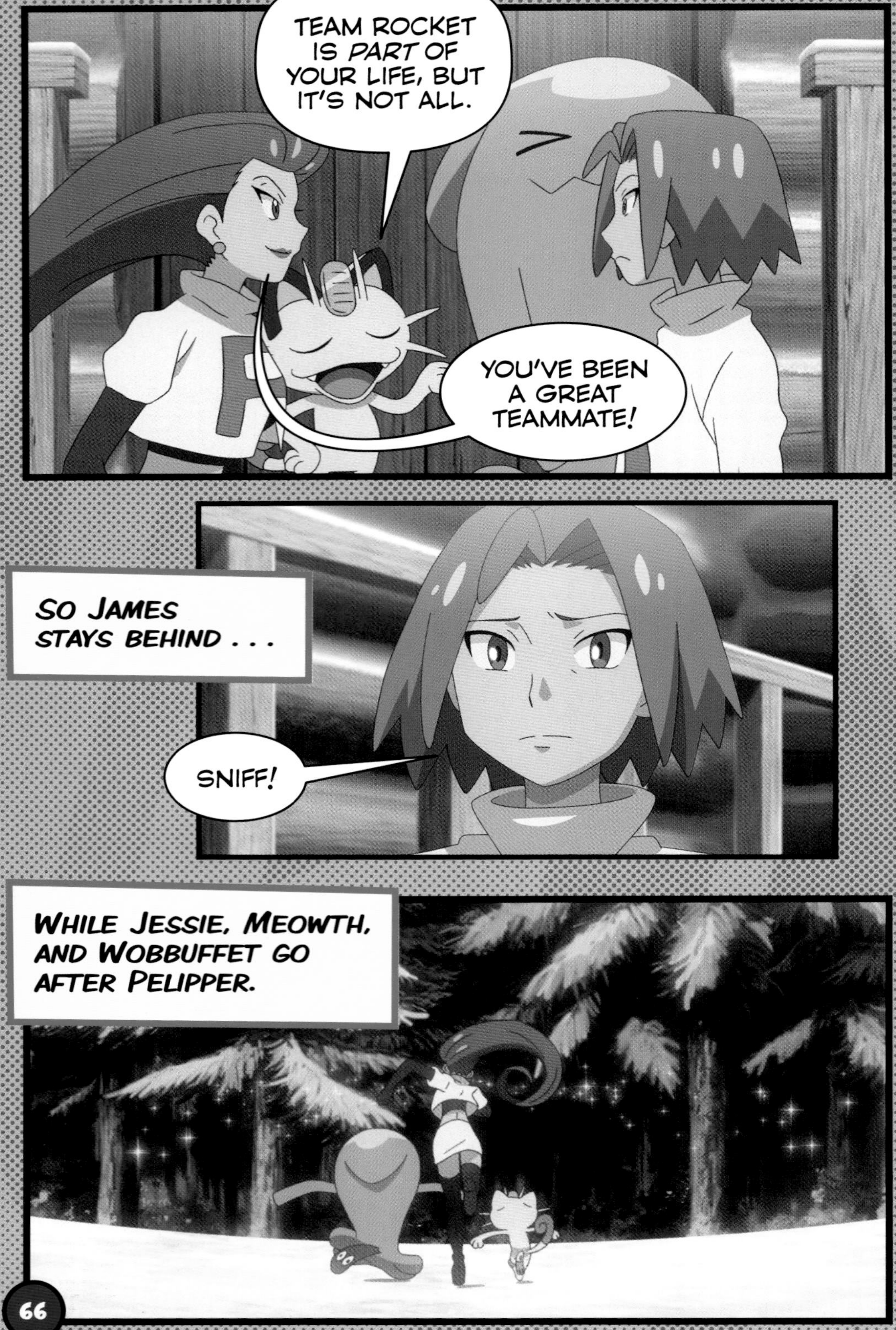
TEAM ROCKET IS PART OF YOUR LIFE, BUT IT'S NOT ALL.
YOU'VE BEEN A GREAT TEAMMATE!
SO JAMES STAYS BEHIND . . .
SNIFF!
WHILE JESSIE, MEOWTH, AND WOBBUFFET GO AFTER PELIPPER.

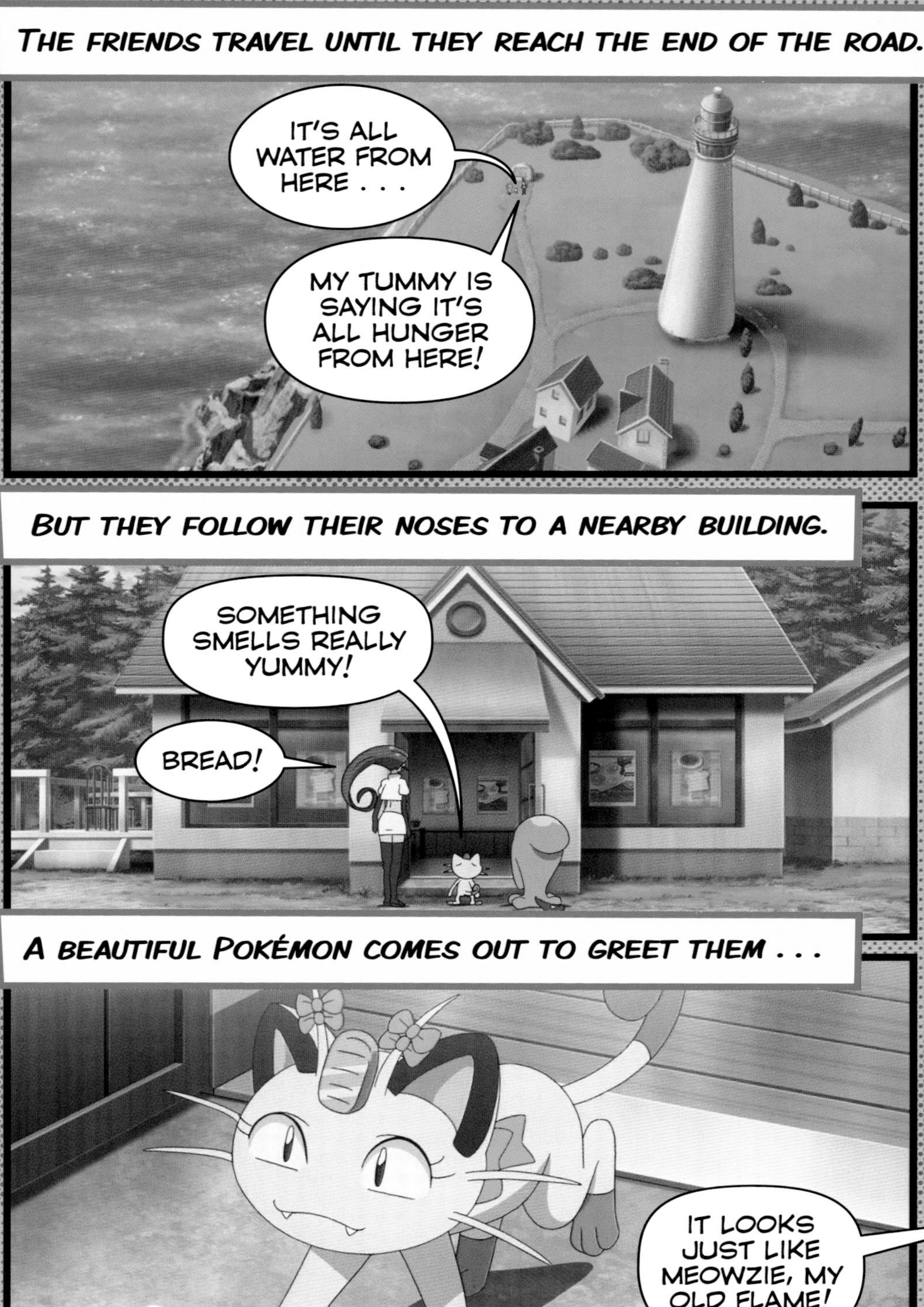
THE FRIENDS TRAVEL UNTIL THEY REACH THE END OF THE ROAD.
IT'S ALL WATER FROM HERE . . .
MY TUMMY IS SAYING IT'S ALL HUNGER FROM HERE!
BUT THEY FOLLOW THEIR NOSES TO A NEARBY BUILDING.
SOMETHING SMELLS REALLY YUMMY!
BREAD!
A BEAUTIFUL POKÉMON COMES OUT TO GREET THEM . . .
IT LOOKS JUST LIKE MEOWZIE, MY OLD FLAME!

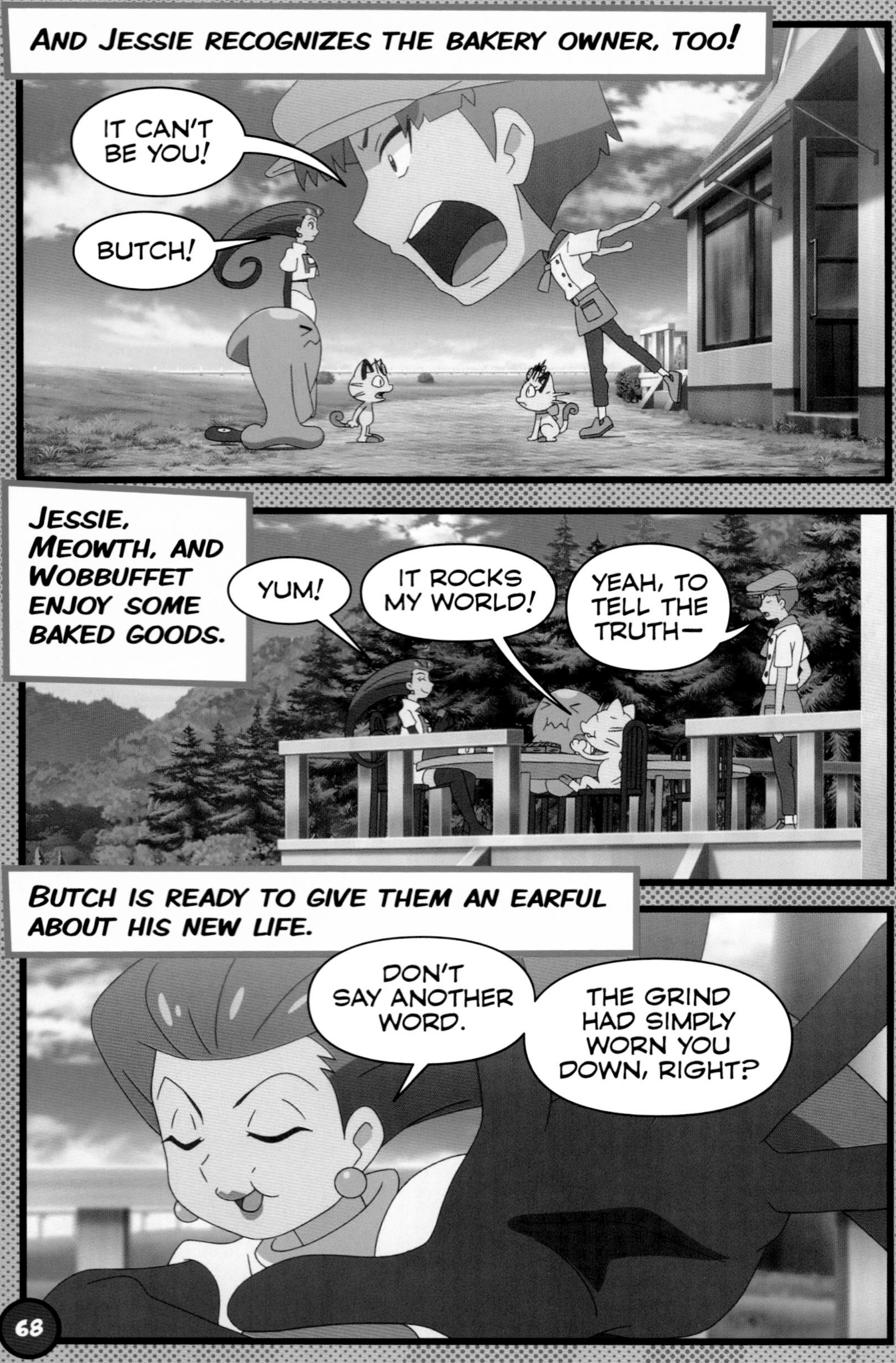
AND JESSIE RECOGNIZES THE BAKERY OWNER, TOO!
IT CAN'T BE YOU!
BUTCH!
JESSIE, MEOWTH, AND WOBBUFFET ENJOY SOME BAKED GOODS.
YUM!
IT ROCKS MY WORLD!
YEAH, TO TELL THE TRUTH—
BUTCH IS READY TO GIVE THEM AN EARFUL ABOUT HIS NEW LIFE.
DON'T SAY ANOTHER WORD.
THE GRIND HAD SIMPLY WORN YOU DOWN, RIGHT?

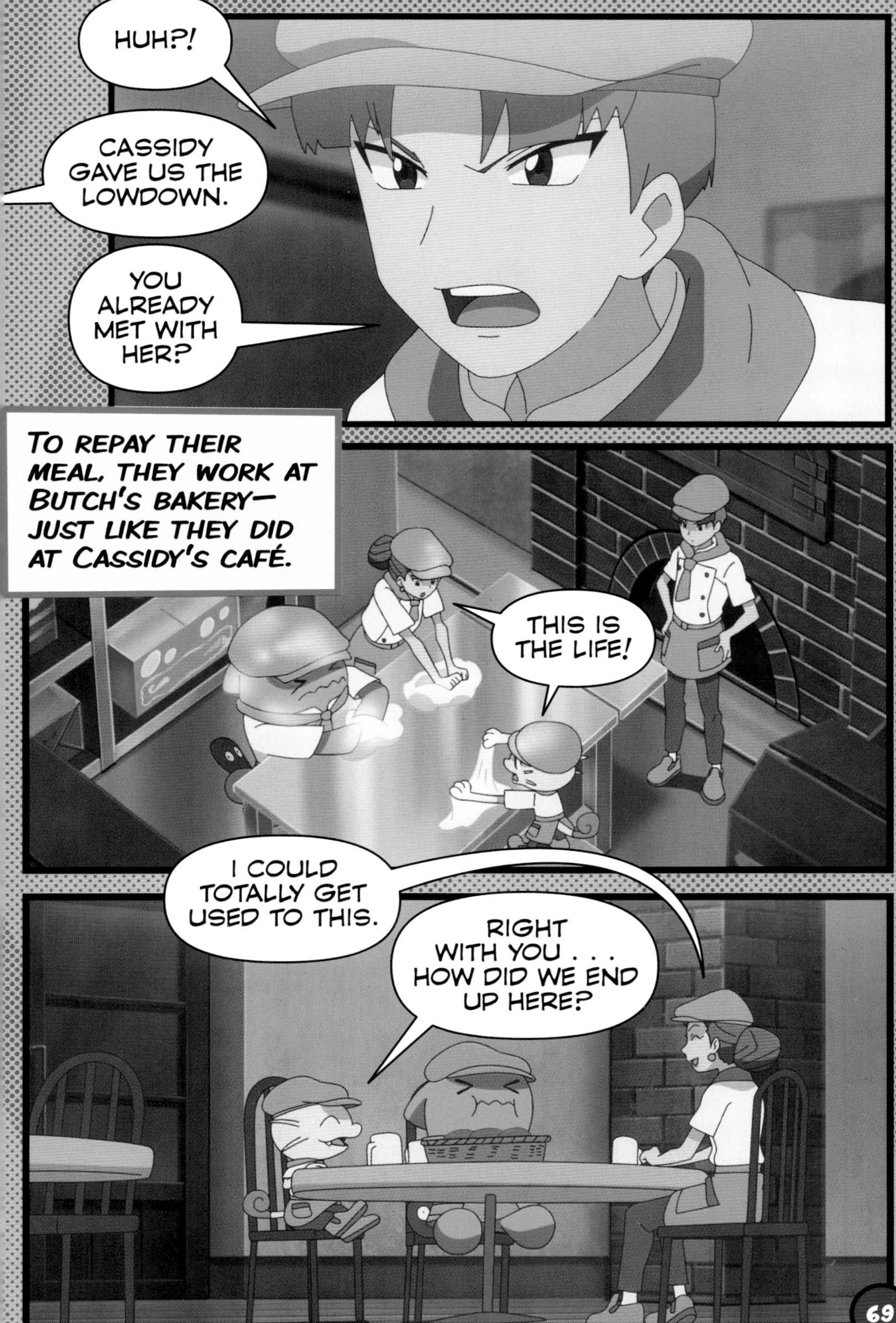
HUH?!
CASSIDY GAVE US THE LOWDOWN.
YOU ALREADY MET WITH HER?
TO REPAY THEIR MEAL, THEY WORK AT BUTCH'S BAKERY—JUST LIKE THEY DID AT CASSIDY'S CAFÉ.
THIS IS THE LIFE!
I COULD TOTALLY GET USED TO THIS.
RIGHT WITH YOU . . . HOW DID WE END UP HERE?

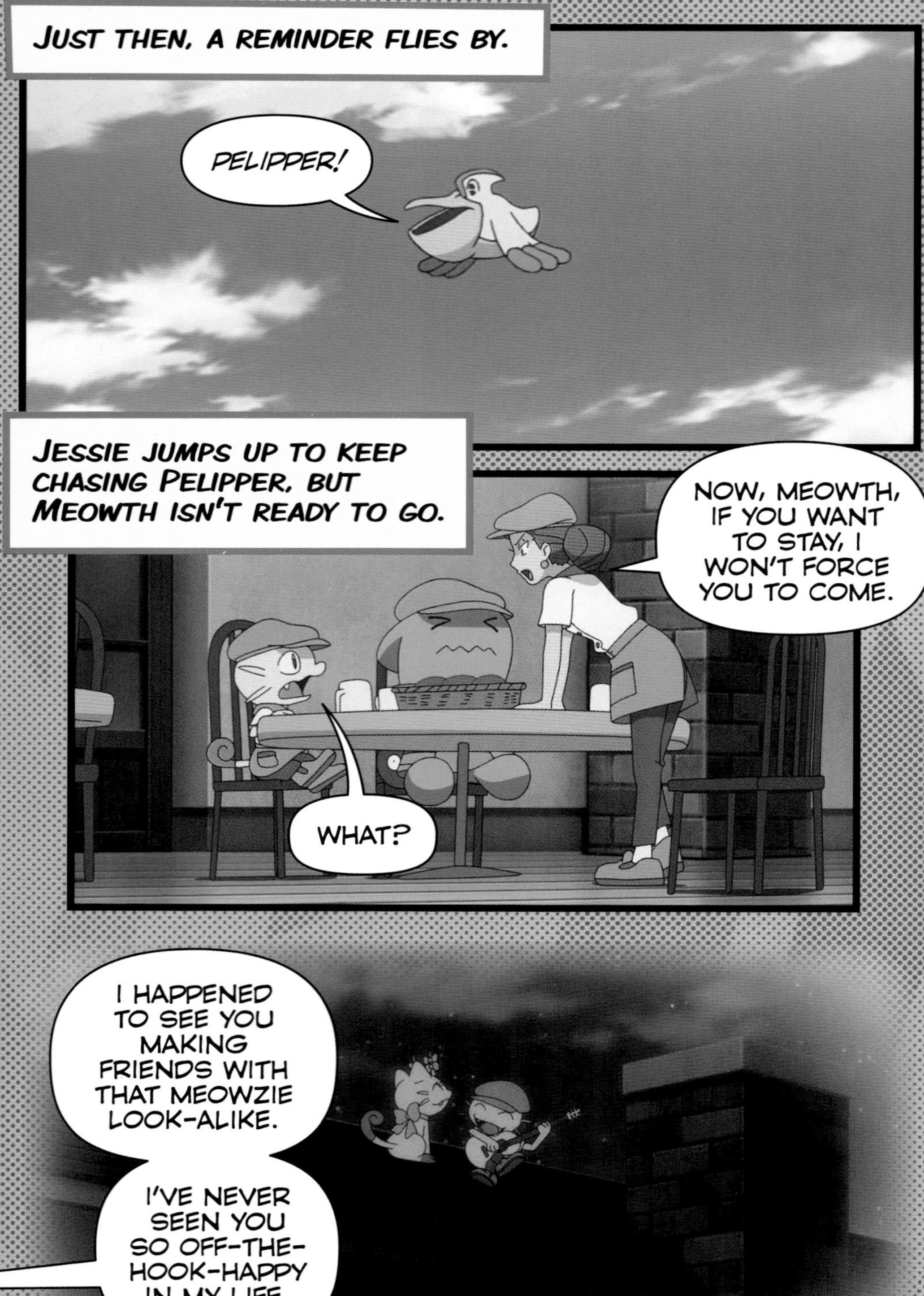
JUST THEN, A REMINDER FLIES BY.
PELIPPER!
JESSIE JUMPS UP TO KEEP CHASING PELIPPER, BUT MEOWTH ISN'T READY TO GO.
NOW, MEOWTH, IF YOU WANT TO STAY, I WON'T FORCE YOU TO COME.
WHAT?
I HAPPENED TO SEE YOU MAKING FRIENDS WITH THAT MEOWZIE LOOK-ALIKE.
I'VE NEVER SEEN YOU SO OFF-THE-HOOK-HAPPY IN MY LIFE.

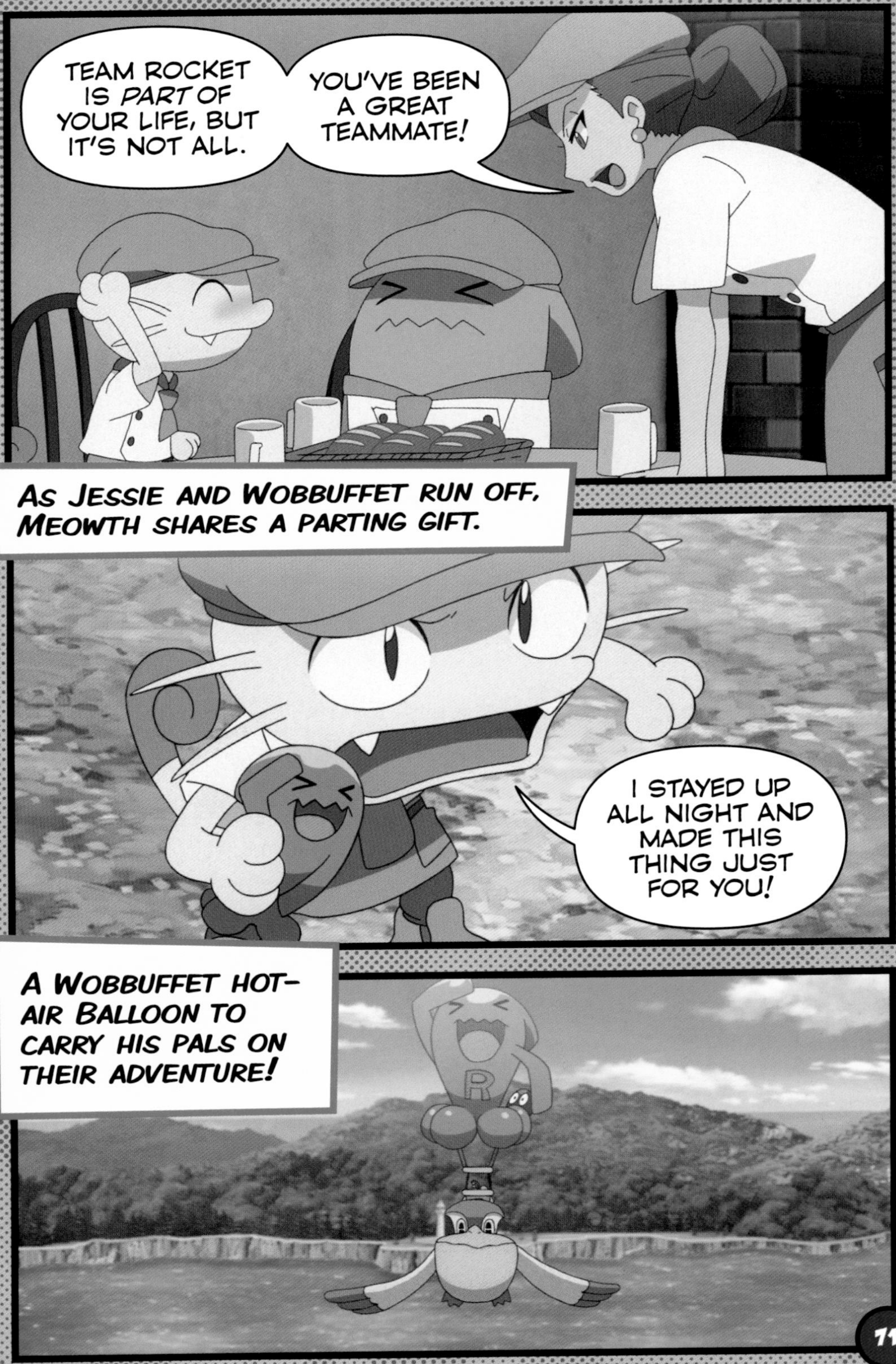
TEAM ROCKET IS PART OF YOUR LIFE, BUT IT'S NOT ALL.
YOU'VE BEEN A GREAT TEAMMATE!
AS JESSIE AND WOBBUFFET RUN OFF, MEOWTH SHARES A PARTING GIFT.
I STAYED UP ALL NIGHT AND MADE THIS THING JUST FOR YOU!
A WOBBUFFET HOT-AIR BALLOON TO CARRY HIS PALS ON THEIR ADVENTURE!

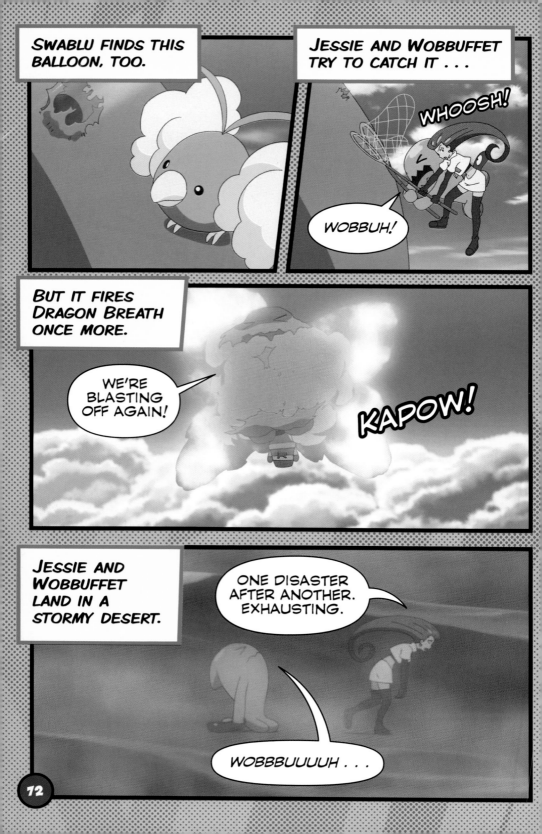

SWABLU FINDS THIS BALLOON, TOO.

JESSIE AND WOBBUFFET TRY TO CATCH IT . . .

WHOOSH!

WOBBUH!

BUT IT FIRES DRAGON BREATH ONCE MORE.

WE'RE BLASTING OFF AGAIN!

KAPOW!

JESSIE AND WOBBUFFET LAND IN A STORMY DESERT.

ONE DISASTER AFTER ANOTHER. EXHAUSTING.

WOBBBUUUUH . . .

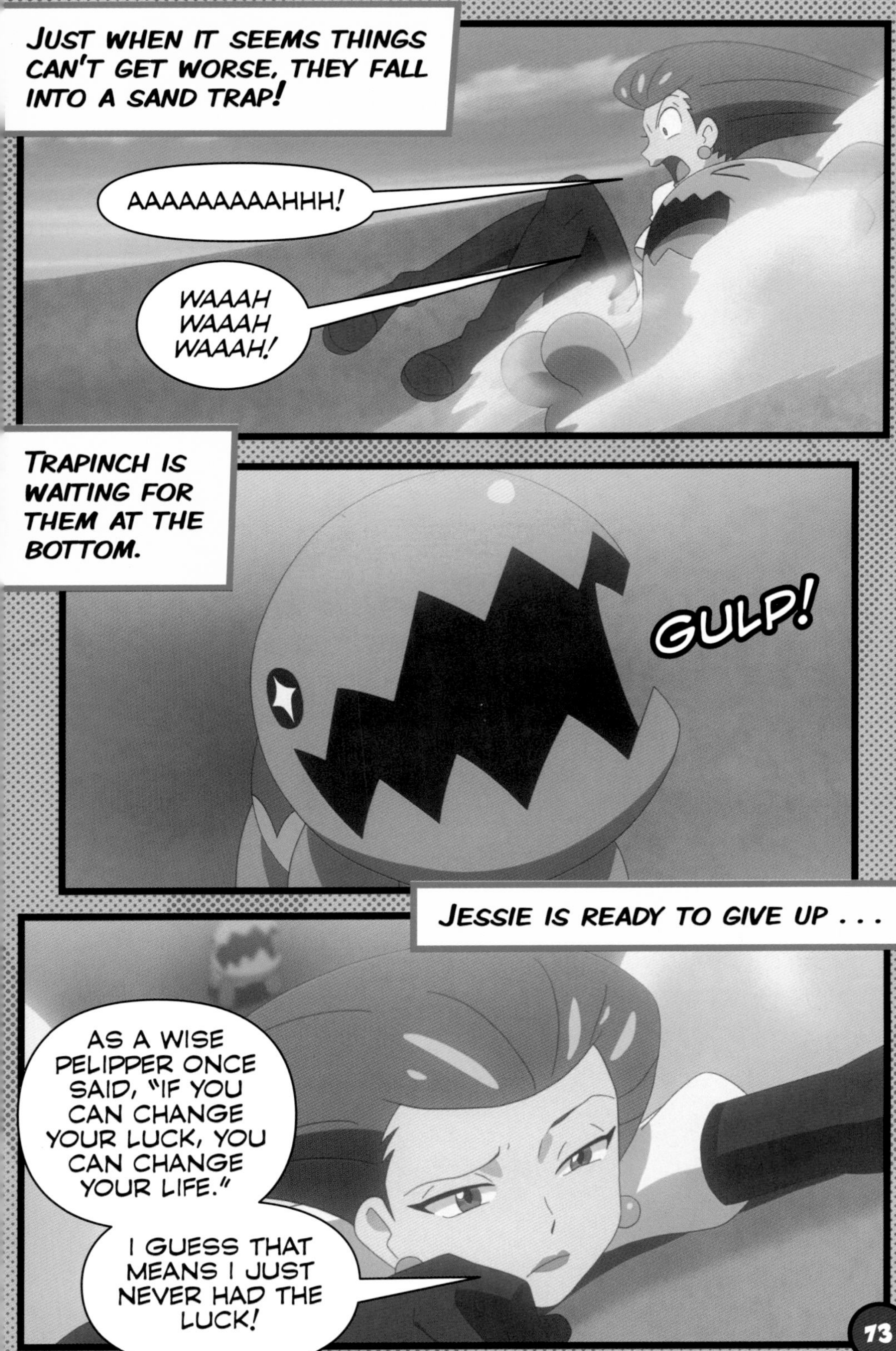
JUST WHEN IT SEEMS THINGS CAN'T GET WORSE, THEY FALL INTO A SAND TRAP!
AAAAAAAAAAHHH!
WAAAH WAAAH WAAAH!
TRAPINCH IS WAITING FOR THEM AT THE BOTTOM.
GULP!
JESSIE IS READY TO GIVE UP . . .
AS A WISE PELIPPER ONCE SAID, "IF YOU CAN CHANGE YOUR LUCK, YOU CAN CHANGE YOUR LIFE."
I GUESS THAT MEANS I JUST NEVER HAD THE LUCK!

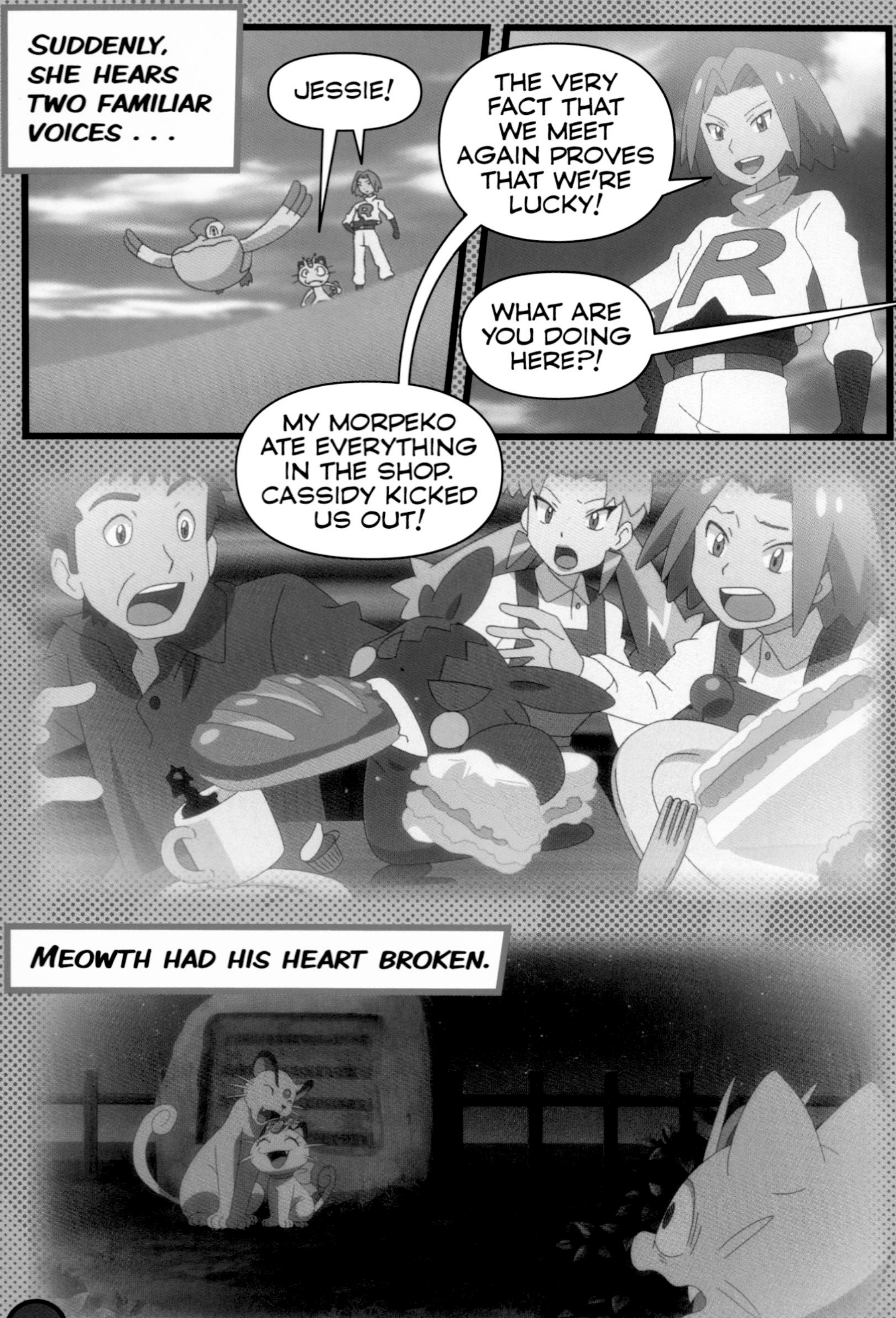
SUDDENLY, SHE HEARS TWO FAMILIAR VOICES . . .
JESSIE!
THE VERY FACT THAT WE MEET AGAIN PROVES THAT WE'RE LUCKY!
WHAT ARE YOU DOING HERE?!
MY MORPEKO ATE EVERYTHING IN THE SHOP. CASSIDY KICKED US OUT!
MEOWTH HAD HIS HEART BROKEN.

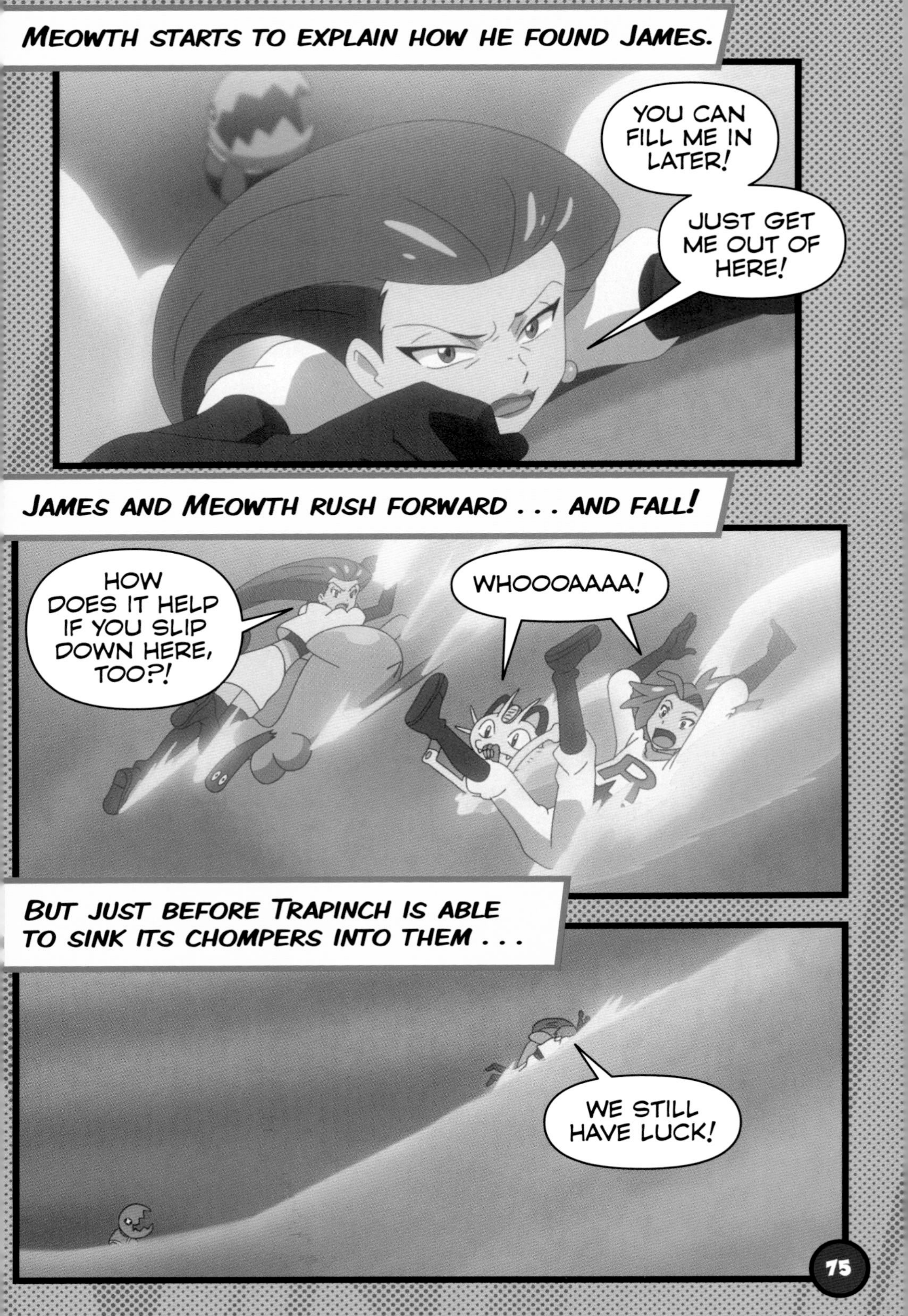
MEOWTH STARTS TO EXPLAIN HOW HE FOUND JAMES.
YOU CAN FILL ME IN LATER!
JUST GET ME OUT OF HERE!
JAMES AND MEOWTH RUSH FORWARD . . . AND FALL!
HOW DOES IT HELP IF YOU SLIP DOWN HERE, TOO?!
WHOOOAAAA!
BUT JUST BEFORE TRAPINCH IS ABLE TO SINK ITS CHOMPERS INTO THEM . . .
WE STILL HAVE LUCK!

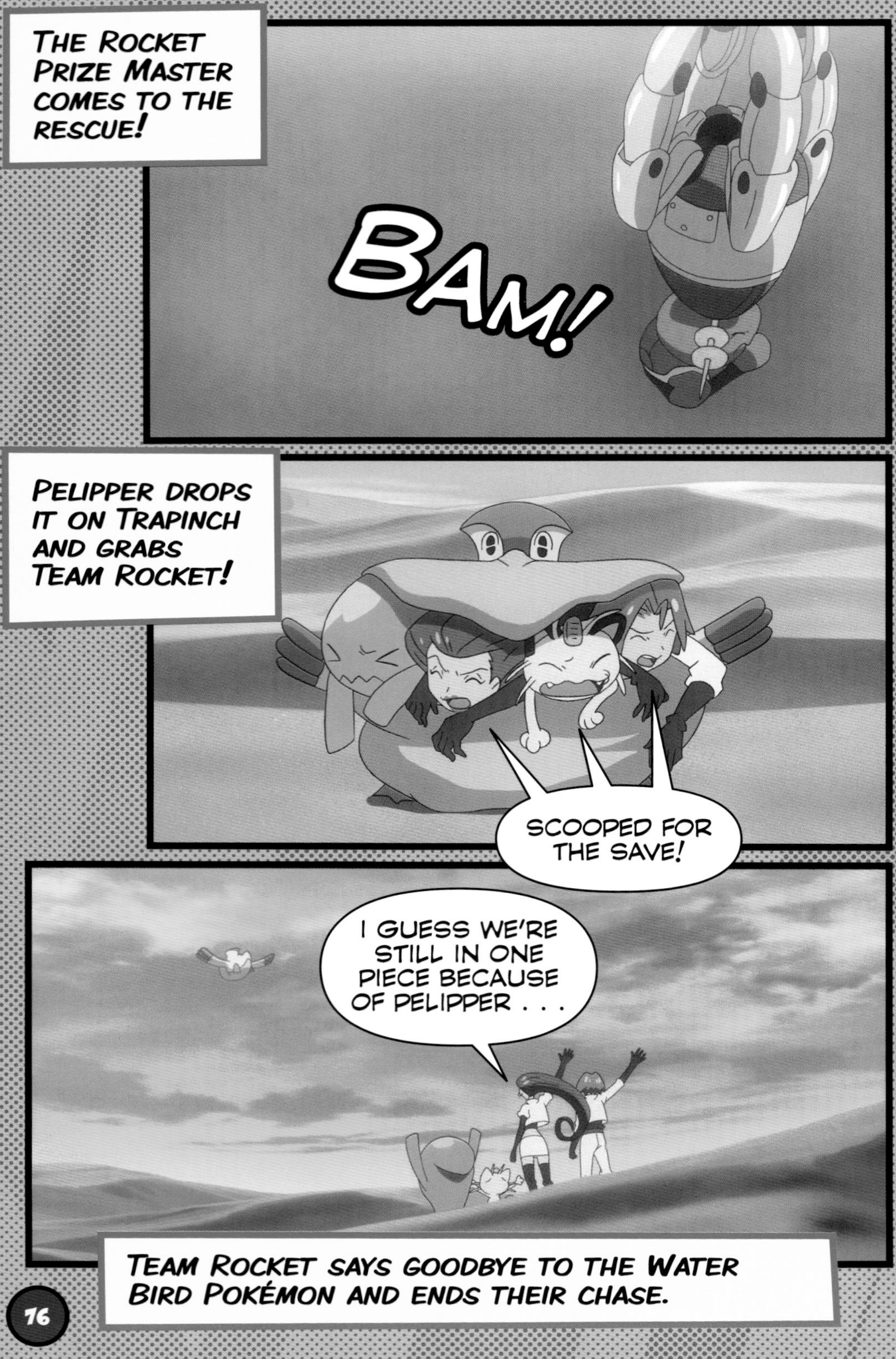
The Rocket Prize Master comes to the rescue!
BAM!
Pelipper drops it on Trapinch and grabs Team Rocket!
Scooped for the save!
I guess we're still in one piece because of Pelipper . . .
Team Rocket says goodbye to the Water Bird Pokémon and ends their chase.

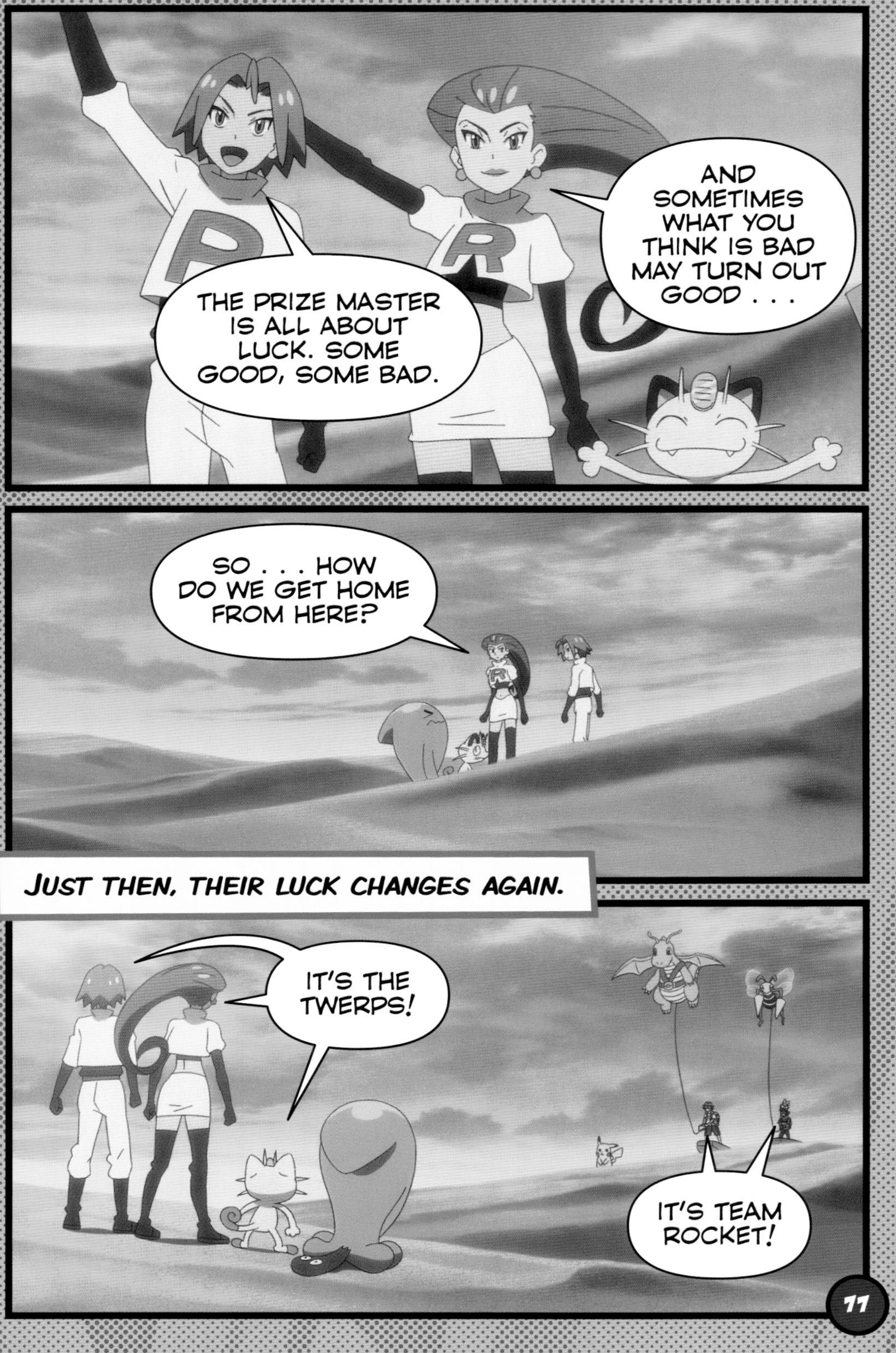
THE PRIZE MASTER IS ALL ABOUT LUCK. SOME GOOD, SOME BAD.
AND SOMETIMES WHAT YOU THINK IS BAD MAY TURN OUT GOOD . . .
SO . . . HOW DO WE GET HOME FROM HERE?
JUST THEN, THEIR LUCK CHANGES AGAIN.
IT'S THE TWERPS!
IT'S TEAM ROCKET!

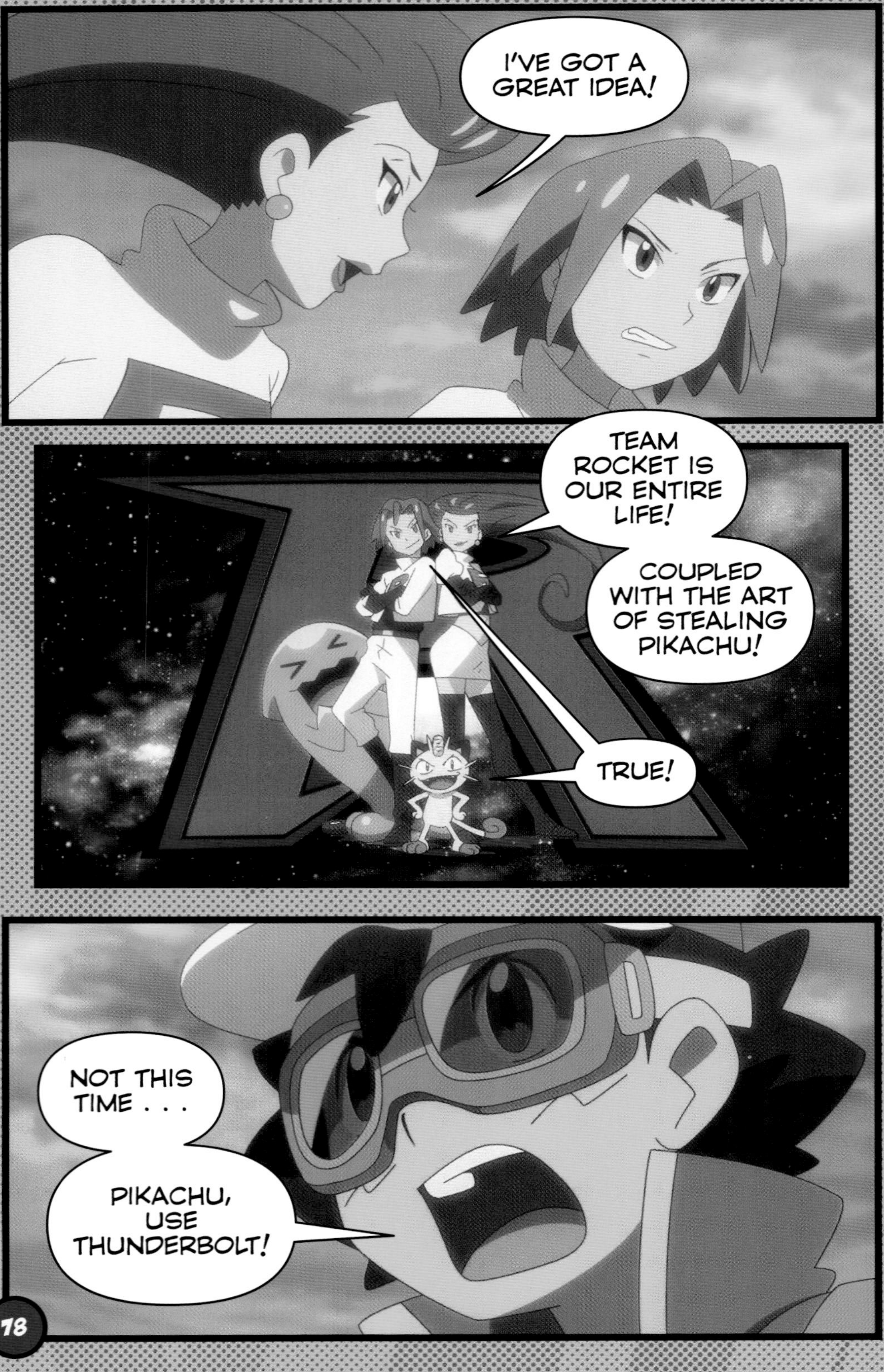

I'VE GOT A GREAT IDEA!
TEAM ROCKET IS OUR ENTIRE LIFE!
COUPLED WITH THE ART OF STEALING PIKACHU!
TRUE!
NOT THIS TIME . . .
PIKACHU, USE THUNDERBOLT!

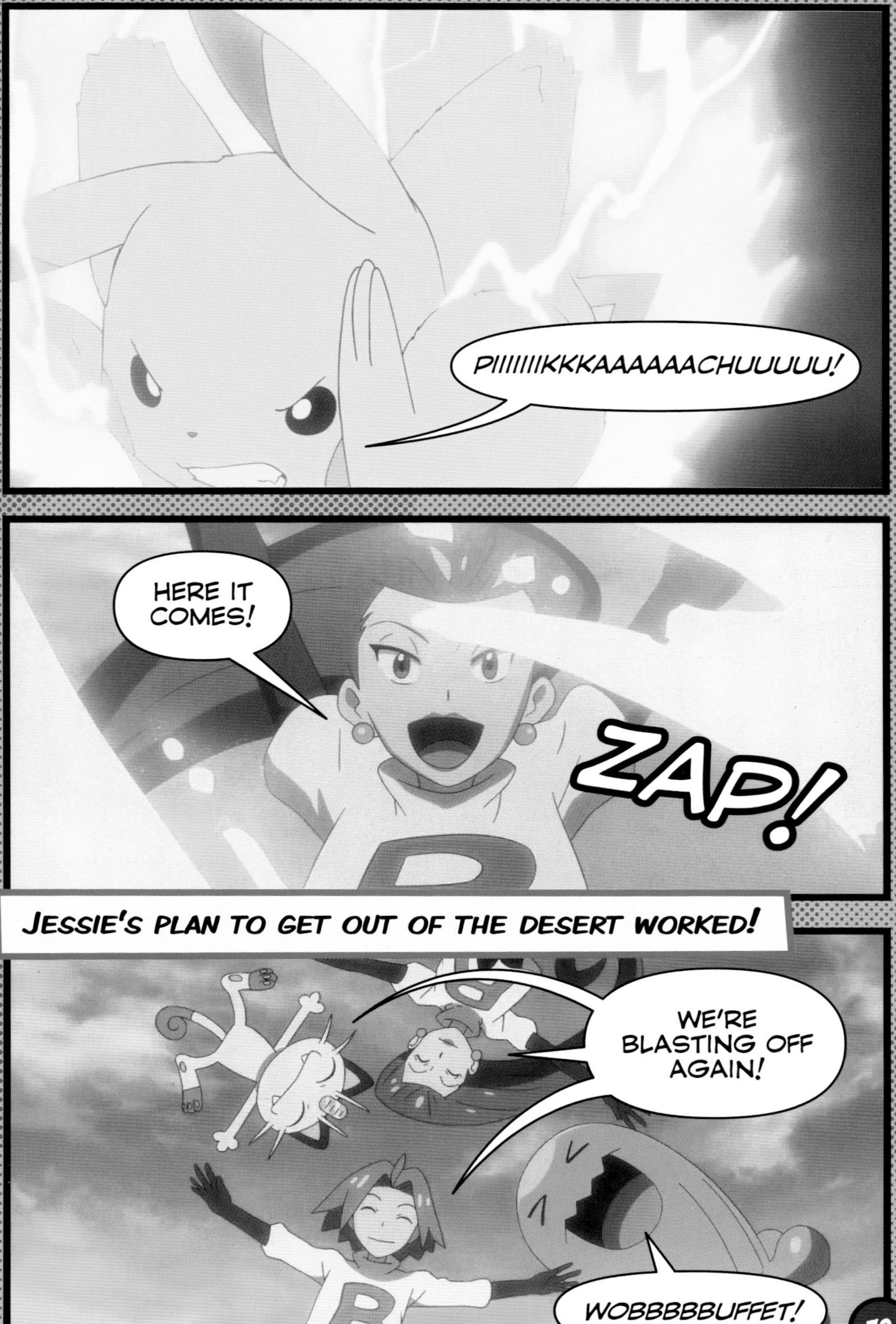
PIIIIIIIKKKAAAAAAACHUUUUUU!
HERE IT COMES!
ZAP!
JESSIE'S PLAN TO GET OUT OF THE DESERT WORKED!
WE'RE BLASTING OFF AGAIN!
WOBBBBBBUFFET!

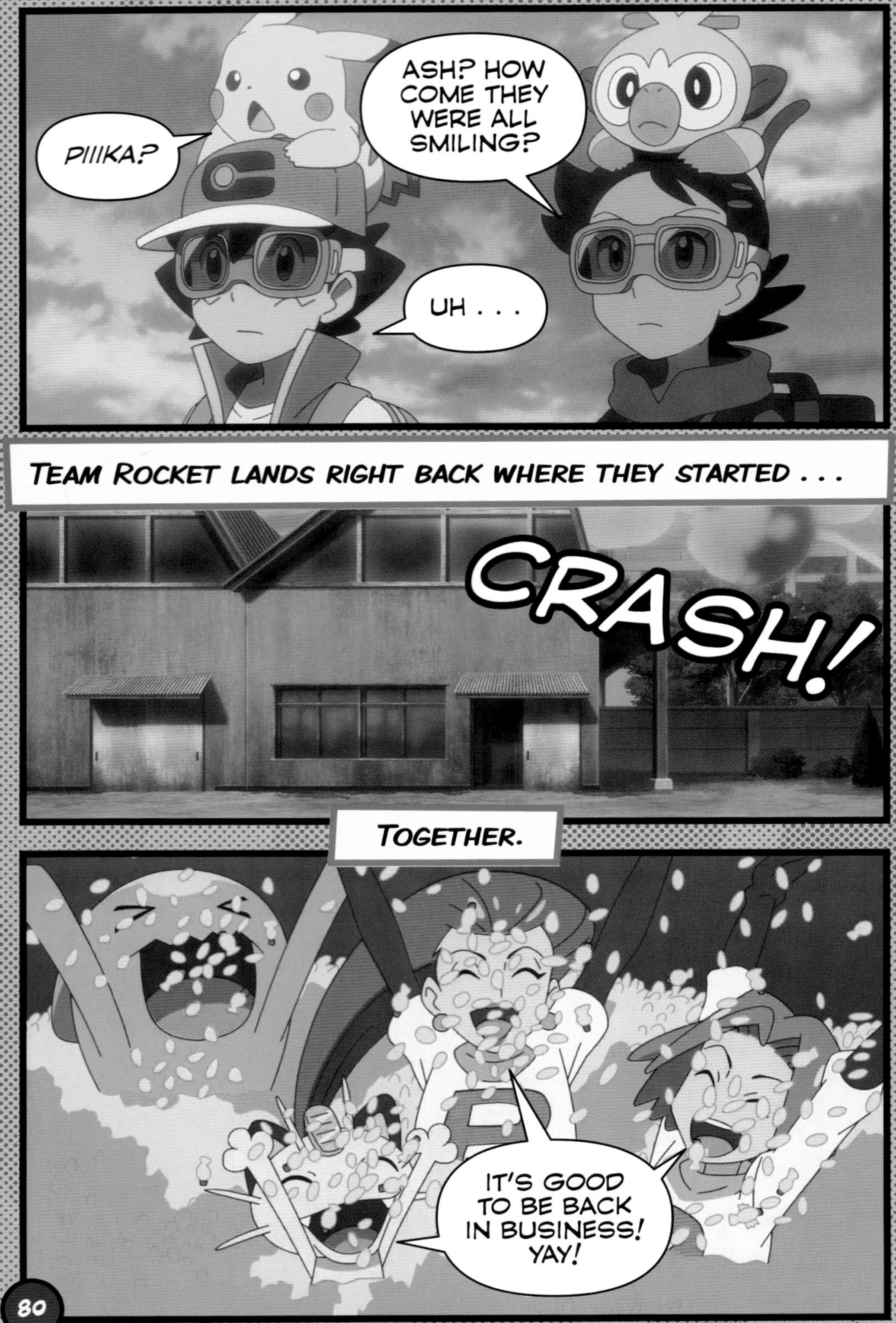
PIIIKA?
ASH? HOW COME THEY WERE ALL SMILING?
UH . . .
TEAM ROCKET LANDS RIGHT BACK WHERE THEY STARTED . . .
CRASH!
TOGETHER.
IT'S GOOD TO BE BACK IN BUSINESS! YAY!